Robert Drewe, the author of widely acclaimed novels and short stories and, more recently, of plays, was born in Victoria but grew up on the coast of Western Australia. *Fortune*, first published in 1986, received international praise and won the fiction prize of the National Book Council Award. His other works of fiction include *The Savage Crows, A Cry in the Jungle Bar, Our Sunshine, The Bay of Contented Men*, which won a Commonwealth Writers' Prize, and his best-selling short story collection, *The Bodysurfers*, which has been adapted for television, radio, film and theatre. His most recently performed play is *South American Barbecue*.

In 1992 Robert Drewe was awarded an Australian Creative Artist's Fellowship by the Prime Minister of Australia.

He lives mainly on the central coast of New South Wales.

Also by Robert Drewe in Picador

THE SAVAGE CROWS
A CRY IN THE JUNGLE BAR
THE BODYSURFERS
THE BAY OF CONTENTED MEN
OUR SUNSHINE

# ROBERT
# DREWE

# FORTUNE

PICADOR
AUSTRALIA

Originally published with the assistance of the Literature Board of the Australia Council

First published 1986 in Picador hardback by Pan Books
(Australia) Pty Ltd
First published 1987 in Picador paperback by Pan Books
(Australia) Pty Ltd
This Picador edition published 1993 by Pan Macmillan
Publishers Australia
a division of Pan Macmillan Australia Pty Limited
63-71 Balfour Street, Chippendale, Sydney

Reprinted 1989, 1990, 1993

National Library of Australia
cataloguing-in-publication data:

Drewe, Robert, 1943-
Fortune
ISBN 0 330 27061 3.
I. Title
A823.3

Printed in Australia by McPherson's Printing Group

*To Bruce Petty*

The opinion expressed by Linda Silver on page 86 on the private investigator and the poet paraphrases that of Sandra Sutherland of San Francisco, whose assistance is gratefully acknowledged.

*

Levinson's view of life expressed on page 200 paraphrases a paragraph by Milan Kundera on page 8 of *The Unbearable Lightness of Being* (Faber and Faber).

*

The author wishes to thank the Literature Board of the Australia Council and the Victorian Ministry for the Arts for their support over different periods during the writing of this novel.

# Author's Note

There is a spot on the map of Western Australia named Thirsty Point but it is an uninhabited promontory situated approximately one hundred miles north, not south, of Perth. The nearest settlement is the small fishing village of Cervantes, named after *Don Quixote's* creator— but only indirectly. The *Cervantes* was an American whaling barque wrecked nearby in 1844.

There was a ship called the *Fortuyn*, owned by the Dutch East India Company and commanded by Pieter Westrik, which sailed on her maiden voyage to Batavia in 1723. However, when this *Fortuyn* left the Cape of Good Hope on 18 January, 1724 she was never heard of again.

R.D.

# Contents

# PART ONE
## From the True

# 1

He came up in such a frenzy, holding the elephant tusk, that he almost brained himself.

He came up under the keel, crashed into it, and laughed nevertheless. He was still laughing, almost drowning, when they pulled him on board. They couldn't believe the elephant tusk.

'A long swim from Africa' they said.

He lay on his back panting and laughing up at the pink streaked sky. The sea stretched tautly around them, the silver skin. On the horizon the sun was a red whale ready to dive.

It made me poetic, he told Caroline Castle. His smile was apologetic. I'd prayed beforehand. Five years is a long time between drinks.

The way her eyes brimmed at his description of this particular afternoon in the Indian Ocean worried him at first. The joyous dusk, the floating sun. The tears halted his expansive gestures.

Go on, she said. Keep talking.

Now his arms described the surprising curve of the elephant tusk. She had an impression of smooth white ivory but of course the tusk was thickened by concretion and encrusted with coral and shellfish.

Laughing, Spargo said to Caroline Castle: They had to believe me this time.

The things he told her that evening in his cups:

The west coast is the best kept secret in the country. You could sell tickets just to see the sun sink into the Indian Ocean. The red whale.

Once I helped excavate a Roman galley off Ibiza, and the western Mediterranean's got nothing on the Indian Ocean. It beats the Med, the Pacific, the bloody Coral Sea.

The mistake everyone makes is they're expecting a wreck to look like a gallant Spanish galleon or something. Lying on the ocean bed with its masts sticking up and its ragged sails fluttering in the current. Underwater bugs, marine termites, chew up the wood and soft stuff in a few years. The ocean bed grows over the rest. All that's left of a sailing ship is the metal, the ballast, the pottery knick-knacks.

(And the ivory, she said. The gold and silver.)

Funny thing, often you find a pair of scissors. A little pair of three-hundred-year-old sterling silver scissors embedded in the reef.

Don't expect to find any skeletons in a wooden-hulled ship.

He told her these things the December night in 1962, the year of parties and celebrations, the year Perth got on the map.

But I'm keeping you from your guests, Spargo said to her on the terrace. All these important people. Astronauts, businessmen, Americans.

The breeze from the river skimmed over them, warm and rich with algae. A clarinet played swing tunes from the host's adolescence.

Don't even think of it, Spargo said to himself that December night.

Just explain the scissors, she said, her nails touching his wrist.

Sailmakers used them. I'm monopolising you.

The Castles' party was the beginning of the story, the part of the story he'd relate first even twenty years later. By then the rest of his chronology was becoming addled. Twenty years later the story was out of his control.

# 2

Journalism couldn't begin to tell the story.

It couldn't cope with the subject, let alone the links between the characters and their ramifications.

In my experience journalism has enough trouble with the libellous, the abstract and the subjective. Its attention span is too short. Anyway, its space limitations prevent the true and continuous tracking of connections. Journalism shies away from psychology. For all its nosy reputation it mostly ignores the private life and rarely sees the larger truth.

And, as if this weren't limiting enough, at the first whiff of trouble personalities intrude, stepping out of the newsprint into the chairman's suite, the general manager's office, the golf club, the yacht club—interfering, threatening, calling in old debts.

That this should still surprise me says something about my provincial innocence. By 1983 I should have realised that journalism reduces most of its stories to political considerations. Matters are defined in terms of where the power lies, who opposes whom or what, where the special interests are.

Nevertheless in 1983 I began blithely writing the story—the story as it stood then—as journalism. I stuck to the publishable facts. I know the publishable facts are never enough but I thought then that straightforward reporting would be adequate to the task.

I can barely remember now what my intentions were. Probably something highfalutin. Perhaps I had in mind a cautionary tale for the late twentieth century obsessive personality. Maybe I wanted to wag an admonishing finger about the dangers of gold fever! I know I wanted to trace the extraordinary procession of events which had followed Spargo's sudden stroke of luck, his wealth and notoriety. At the same time I was urgently trying to justify to myself my return to journalism, and had decided that the profession (craft? trade?) existed to tell stories such as Spargo's.

I'd been on an investigative binge since my return, the usual idealistic reporter's crusade against corrupt authority and inept bureaucracy. Certainly I wanted the bad cop, the blundering politician, the union leader on the take. I wasn't too blasé to take up the little man caught in the cogs. But what I was really looking for was the doomed hero, the thwarted genius, the top seed put down by cruel circumstance.

Obviously I was hoping to put my own case.

I was in a bad way. This was my situation: after fifteen years as a reporter in Perth, Western Australia, I had left newspapers two years before to write a novel. *My novel.* Ten years in the anticipation. At last I could manage it. I was brimming with confidence and long-service pay. Of course I implied to my colleagues that the break was final. They wished me well and detested me. I was thirty-five and starting a new life of happiness and rich creativity. A publisher liked my synopsis. As the farewell party hangovers receded I began this new regimen of discipline and inspiration. I tiptoed up to the doorstep of Literature. I began, slowly, to write.

But—and it still bewilders me to recall how the time flew—my money and my imagination seemed to run out simultaneously. One morning—sharper, brighter, bluer than the rest; not a cloud or a nuance or an ambiguity in the dry air—they had simply disappeared. Trickled away. I borrowed more money to keep writing and then became too worried to write. In an icy moment I doubted whether I had the emotional wherewithal ever to complete a novel.

So I returned to newspapers. But not to the provincial press of Perth. Unwilling to face my old smirking colleagues and determined to salvage some professional self-esteem, I moved east and took a job on the *Sydney Morning Herald*. At least back home this was seen as a rise in station (though I now had to take a drop in salary). However, the uprooting, the disruption, the unfamiliar big city, all fed my disorder. I was angry at myself for giving in and resentful at having my literary 'career' stopped in its tracks. Had I returned to journalism against my will—as I told myself—or had I willingly succumbed to the by-line more easily won?

And now I had to prove myself as a Sydney reporter, to overcome the usual prejudice against the boondocks and the extra count against me (revealed in an unguarded moment at the pub) of being a 'writer'. In other words a dilettante. This goaded me into feats of such journalistic derring-do, such hectic ambulance-chasing, that I arrived home each night too over-stimulated or enervated to do my own writing. More than ever I questioned my ability to write a novel. The tension overflowed into my domestic life and flooded everything.

I welcomed the Spargo story. The Spargo story had certain parallels. Under the surface, as it were.

# 3

There is a fact of life in a country with a small population: everyone over thirty knows everyone else. Either you have grown up with them or played sports against them or taken them to dances or made love to them. And now there they are—in government or in jail or anchoring the television news.

The sensation of knowing everyone is enhanced in the more isolated and self-contained cities, the sorts of places where the newspaper's birth, death and matrimonial notices are still pored over each morning; the sorts of places like Perth, where Spargo and I grew up and where I first interviewed him when he discovered the wreck of the Dutch merchantman *Fortuyn* in 1962.

In such places individual paths seem to follow each other, crossing and re-crossing over the years, increasing the chances of extraordinary coincidences occurring. People and events collide and glance off each other in a ricochet effect.

An interesting fact was apt to occur to me during 1983 when my energy was in reporting and my bitter heart was in my unfinished novel: whereas fiction turns up its nose at coincidence, life insists upon it. Life's tendency to ricochet is why life, in its spasmodic narrative rhythms, more closely resembles a comic strip, say, than it does a novel.

Ricocheting off one another, knowing 'everyone', can be very comforting, of course. It reinforces one's sense of security. It suits the egalitarian mode of this country to regard prominent people in a familiar or proprietorial way, even if one has barely met them.

But it also carries risks. There is the danger of not seeing beyond the cosiness of the coterie, of wrongly imagining one belongs with the insiders, the movers and shakers.

Where people have important friends there is always the danger they will call on them to act.

# 4

In Sydney in February 1983 Spargo appeared one day in the small glass and wood-panelled office I shared in the newspaper's features department. A young, nervous woman was with him, and an older, weather-beaten man hovered in the background.

Five minutes earlier Spargo had telephoned from the security guard's cubicle downstairs after the guard had stopped him on his way up to see me.

'Give this gentleman the word,' he said. 'Inform him our working relationship goes back twenty years.'

Our 'working relationship' was actually quite tenuous. Since 1962 I had spoken to him perhaps twenty times, mostly during 1964 and 1965 when I had covered the convoluted legal wrangles he was beginning to attract.

On his first day in court in 1964 we had walked from the Supreme Court to the Palace Hotel for a drink at the end of the day. His face was still red from the polite humiliations of the law. A warm soft rain fell on St. George's Terrace. Office workers lined neatly for buses. Steam rose from the road.

'Who do they think they're dealing with?' Spargo said.

He had been in the news intermittently since then, but chiefly in the local papers. When his name did make the national news, as it had lately, old hometown memories and associations (my feeling of knowing 'everyone') made it jump out of the mass of type and grab my attention, though the latest headline, EXPLORER CONSPIRED TO BOMB EX-WIFE, SAY POLICE would surely have accomplished that in any case.

So I had read of his recent arrest in Sydney, and of his release, against police opposition, on high bail; read also of the bail granted one Rosanna McMahon, his alleged co-conspirator (and '*de facto* wife' as the papers would continue to describe her), presumably the young, uneasy woman who was now biting her nails and glancing skittishly around my office.

The man in the background was also anxious. He was introduced as Ken Marriott, a retired businessman of some sort (marine supplies, sporting goods), a friend who had 'stood by' them.

After the company Spargo had kept in the sixties and seventies these two seemed unpolished and awkward. The woman was only nineteen or twenty, and thick-waisted under a plain cotton sun dress. Nibbling at her cuticles she looked like a country girl from a distant state.

A victim, I thought.

No Caroline Castle, I thought.

'I have an interesting proposition,' Spargo said.

He wanted the newspaper to pay his legal fees. He said he had court cases piled up in several states and his bail money was tied up. In return he offered his 'story'. He was quite unabashed about this offer; not a hint of irony or self-consciousness showed in his steady gaze.

His gall and confidence rocked me. I almost smiled. He was presuming, and the presumption was mirrored in the deferential manner of Rosanna and Marriott, that he did, in fact, have a 'story'. In other words that he was famous and that his life was interesting enough to sell newspapers.

He must have considered my reaction because he changed his tune somewhat. 'Going public is my only hope,' he said.

His story, he intimated, was fascinating if not heroic. He seemed to see himself as an amalgam of Jacques Cousteau, Columbus and Dreyfus. He had an axe to grind and then he wanted to wield it. He wanted to reveal corruption in high places, name important names. There was even a bonus for the newspaper's color supplement and its associated magazines and television station: he'd take cameramen and reporters around the coastline and show them the thirty or forty shipwrecks he had discovered and kept under wraps.

'This is a big island with a lot of secrets,' he said. 'I'm talking about everything from Roman galleys to Phoenician triremes. These could turn our history upside down.'

I said it would make history if this newspaper ever paid out money to anyone. It disliked making deals for news. He would have to tell me his 'story' first, show me some proof of his allegations—whatever they were— before I could pass on his proposition.

'What about conspiring to murder your ex-wife, for a start?' I said then.

His expression didn't change. Perhaps his cheeks flushed slightly. 'A twisting of words,' he said. 'A frame-up.'

'But a serious charge.'

'Listen, she's still walking around as happy as Larry. If it was a serious charge I wouldn't be out on bail.'

I said I couldn't promise anything, but I was vaguely, parochially, curious. Next day I brought a photographer to Marriott's flat in Drummoyne where Spargo and

Rosanna were staying under the terms of their bail agreement, reporting to the local police three times a week until their committal hearing.

I remember going through the motions. I remember Spargo delivering a long rambling spiel in the sun on Marriott's quarry-tiled patio with its narrow harbour view up the Parramatta River. I remember the bored photographer gazing across the water.

My notes from that morning quote Spargo as saying that many people were after him, from the government down. The police in three states were in league against him, also the Federal police, the public service and some very powerful individuals. Naturally Marriott's phone was tapped; he had also received, and taped, several threatening calls.

'I'm tired of constantly looking behind me,' Spargo said. 'Conspiracy-to-murder, it's a joke.' What had happened was that the police had eventually found someone with a sufficient grudge against him who would say that he and Rosanna had asked him to help bomb Natalie Spargo's house. 'It's as simple as that. They can always get you on something,' he said matter-of-factly.

'I'll have to see some evidence of all this,' I said. 'You know the legal problems. This is all *sub judice*.'

*Paranoid*, I thought.

'Put it this way,' he said. 'Ever been stopped ten times in one day for minor traffic offences? A broken filament in your tail-light? Dirty licence plate? The bastards can always find something.'

'Like conspiracy-to-murder?'

The photographer wouldn't catch my eye. He was fascinated by a tourist ferry passing on the harbour.

'They say they'll get him,' Rosanna said nervously. 'A car accident or something.' She smoothed her frock over her rounded stomach. She was pregnant: four or five months. That as well.

Marriott's thin silent wife brought us coffee.

'It's scandalous what they're doing to him,' Marriott ventured, dunking a biscuit.

'I'm getting all the documentation together,' Spargo said. 'To prove my case.'

'Good, that's what we need.'

'Do you want to take the pictures down by the water?' he asked.

Old habits die hard.

# 5

Pictures were taken.

It's not polite if a photographer is present to leave an assignment without taking one or two photographs. The subject feels less than newsworthy—insignificant. Also the photographer likes to protect himself. Perhaps the subject will be struck by lightning five minutes after he leaves.

The same principle applies to reporting. It's polite and self-protective to take a few notes even if there is no intention of filing a story.

Get the names, ages, addresses, occupations. Lesson One: *Who? When? Where? Why? How?*

I am looking now at the photograph—which was not published or even printed then but which was widely published later—that the photographer took that morning by the harbour at Drummoyne.

The crown of the Harbour Bridge is a faint curve in the distance. Small boats sit at their moorings in the Parramatta River, which flows around and behind Spargo. He grins on its muddy tidal shore. His face shows a high colour, even in monochrome. But he looks healthy for his age and state of anxiety—rational, not noticeably paranoid. He is leaning nonchalantly against the harbour wall holding a big polythene mooring buoy in his hand.

Photographers like props. A press photograph is a tiny frozen performance. Their favourite indoor props are the telephone and the pen, often both together. Outdoors, depending on context, the larger scale requires a building, machinery, at a pinch a tree, best of all an animal or child. At Drummoyne the mooring buoy was the closest prop at hand.

At Drummoyne for thirty seconds there was spontaneous collusion between the photographer and the subject.

The photographer said, 'Just hold that buoy, will you?'

Simultaneously, Spargo picked up the buoy and slid his glasses off and into his shirt pocket.

'Better,' the photographer agreed. 'One more.'

The photograph in front of me proves the lightning strike principle. So does the item it is illustrating, a story I wrote urgently for the news pages a week later. The same photograph—Spargo holding the mooring buoy— came to be used again six weeks later, and many more times over the next two years.

I was grateful at the time for my notes of the Drummoyne meeting. The information for this news item came from a frantic Rosanna. She said Spargo had been abducted. There had been a phone call purporting to come from the Federal police asking him to meet them, and now he had disappeared. 'They've taken him,' she said. 'He said they would.' The Federal police denied contacting him; the State police had him listed as a bail absconder. Either way, he had vanished.

From that point this became a story which defied Lesson One. It flew in the face of the Golden Rule. It changed tack, altered shape, wilfully added and subtracted characters. The constants were very few.

I sensed the story was leading inevitably to a dramatic

conclusion but it veered away from the constraints of journalism and refused to signal its route. At one time there may have been a *Who?* and a *When?* and perhaps even a *Where?*

At no point in the coming months, however, was there a definite *Why?* or *How?*

# 6

The magistrate who would commit Spargo and Rosanna for trial for conspiracy to murder would later describe the case as the 'most peculiar' he had presided over.

Their barrister at the trial would say to me: 'This case has got everything but the elephants.'

I was getting an inkling of this when I wrote the news story about his disappearance in February 1983. But I had badly underestimated how far Spargo was out of kilter by then. I was influenced by *his* props: the pregnant girlfriend left behind, the taped threats against him, the high bail money he had posted, not to mention the treasure I imagined he had stashed away somewhere. To me he had everything to lose by running away.

Consequently my story leaned slightly towards the abduction theory. I quoted Rosanna McMahon's fears that he would be killed. I quoted from the taped 'threats' against him, while also quoting the police as saying they had 'no information to suggest' he had been abducted. By the time I had outlined his battles with authority all over the country and underlined his role in West Australian folk-lore, my pen-picture of 'Australia's most famous underwater explorer, Don Spargo,' showed almost a classic case. It was almost pure in its self-evident truths: gold causes malign disarray; modern society abhors the individual.

I was slightly off the track. Axioms could not be said to apply entirely.

In 1983 I was too far away from Perth's efficient rumour mills, and too selectively cynical, to take into account such journalistic intangibles as romantic despair. I could identify easily enough with sublimation of ego, with simple chagrin, with someone having had bulky obstacles thrown in the path of ambition. But I hadn't enough understanding of heroic madness, of erratic martyrdom, of the willingness to go over the edge.

What sort of would-be artist did this make me?

What sort of journalist for that matter? I'd been used by Spargo, set up by his suggestion of a deal and by my observation of his situation. Any story I would write (did in fact write) would (and probably did) help his getaway. He had jumped bail. He'd sacrificed everything—Rosanna, his bail money, whatever he retained of his treasure, perhaps a favourable trial outcome.

Anyway, six weeks later a heavily-armed team of police arrested him in a road ganger's shack in the desert at Boondie (population twenty-five) in central Australia. My first thought on hearing this news was that he couldn't have positioned himself further from the sea. He had hidden himself in the very centre of the land mass. The police said they had seized a .22 rifle and six sticks of gelignite in the raid, but he surrendered without a fight—a physical fight, at least. He did fight an extended court battle, as usual, against extradition to New South Wales, alleging flamboyantly that it would imperil his life to send him back to Sydney. However, the police gritted their teeth and went through the proper legal processes and five days later he was in Long Bay jail.

Some sections of Perth society could have predicted as much back in the sixties.

# 7

Twenty years ago provincial cities like Perth were even more self-absorbed and gossipy than they are today. Certainly in 1962 when Spargo eventually found his treasure that December afternoon lying at only four fathoms and overlaid with coral-encrusted elephant tusks, it seemed to the visiting Leon Levinson that every cab driver and barmaid and barber in town—to hear them talk of him— was his closest friend.

Ironically, Spargo was just beginning to move in more exalted circles. At the Castles' party he and Levinson were the 'celebrity' guests. Levinson's memory of the evening was vivid. This was a new race of people and he observed them with curiosity. Everyone laughed a lot and drank with gusto. Many of the male guests— business, Establishment types—surprised him by drinking beer instead of spirits. Their wives sipped brandy and ginger ale from glasses rimmed with frosted sugar. Colourful fruits and plastic straws poked merrily out of glasses. Warm yeasty air flowed over them all.

Levinson floated with fatigue and incomprehension among these tanned and eager folk, nodding and smiling into their frank faces while they swirled around him. The men bantered and snorted like successful men anywhere, but the code of their accents was impregnable. Their chattering wives displayed their tanned chests and shoulders with great boldness but no provocation, unselfconsciously hitching up their strapless fronts while they gossiped.

Studying their suntans, Levinson noticed that the seemingly uniform brownness was often really a stippled arrangement of thousands of closely packed freckles.

Halfway through the evening Spargo and their hostess came up and began babbling. Bright-eyed, Caroline Castle introduced them and then left them together. The excitement of Spargo's recent discovery was in his eyes as he followed her progress back across the terrace. He recklessly waved a glass of beer at her smooth departing back.

At this stage the phrase 'rapture of the deep' occurred to Levinson, both in relation to Spargo and to the condition in which he found himself.

This stranger Spargo was rhapsodising about the grandeurs of the deep, his thick arms making unlikely fluttery artistic motions in the air, while cornering him on a terrace overlooking a black, still river at the end of the earth.

All Levinson could do was nod and float while his soul was still in New York or Budapest or Pisa or wherever.

The river was called the Swan.

He had arrived that morning from a wintry New York after an interminable flight via already forgotten stopovers. But although exhausted and disoriented he was not unhappy. He loved to arrive in a new town and face new situations. In a foreign place, for a moment, life still had the air of fiction. He felt like a character in a novel or a movie. Then he adapted, strangeness became familiarity and the sensation vanished. Admittedly he was a geographical snob. To find himself on a balmy summer evening in the world's most far-flung city seemed to him so extraordinary an achievement as to make him, sipping his cold lager, truly famous in his own eyes.

This fellow Spargo enunciated very loudly and clearly to him, as if to a baby or an imbecile. Or a foreigner. He didn't take it as rudeness though. Spargo had a message to impart.

'Leon, I am unstoppable.'

# 8

In Perth in 1962 he had a lapel tag saying 'Official NASA Artist Leon J. Levinson'.

He had sheafs of letters of introduction from everyone from John Glenn to Henry R. Luce.

He was on the *Life* payroll but had been seconded to the space program since 1961 when he'd been invited to be inspired by the flights of Mercury. The artistic results were periodically displayed by the *Life* editors, who by this stage were seeking their own inspiration on how best to illustrate imaginatively the long-running saga of the astronauts which had so captivated their chairman.

As far as Levinson was concerned—he revealed to me, off the record—the novelty had quickly worn off after Shepard's and Grissom's flights.

On the record, he said that in his opinion the Florida launching might better have intrigued Salvador Dali 'as the magical stage where cosmogony met art'.

On the record, he said that the surprisingly slow, portentous levitation of the rocket 'smacked of Flash Gordon'.

Off the record, he said he'd been more interested in the honky-tonks around Cape Canaveral.

Very much on the record he said that 'thanks to the good-natured citizens of Perth,' John Glenn's orbital flight on 20 February, 1962 had extended his beat considerably.

Learning that Glenn's Mercury capsule was to pass directly overhead that night, the people of Perth had chosen to defy the meteorological and municipal sceptics and light a greeting to him.

The city turned on all its lights. Every living-room, kitchen and street lamp blazed. One hundred and twenty-five miles up Glenn saw the glow, remarked on it from his capsule, and thanked the people for their gesture.

Henry Luce had also seen the glow. It was suggested that Levinson might like to visit this warm-hearted, astronaut-welcoming, America-loving town. Someone from NASA remarked, winking, that Gordon Cooper had greatly enjoyed the social life there while manning the space tracking station for Glenn's flight and doing a little astronaut public relations. Someone else said that Perth was the most remote western city in the world. This gave it more curiosity value. *Life* liked the whole idea of Australia, and this was Australia in essence.

Levinson paid heed. He supposed he was lucky that Luce still liked his drawings; at least the *Life* editors thought he liked them, which amounted to the same thing. He suspected that the founder believed he was a refugee from communism and thus to be encouraged. Whatever the reason, *Life* had made his life apt for him.

I was certainly envious of his life and, as a first-year reporter, new to candour in my interview subjects. I wrote that he travelled, 'inspired by news, nature, cities, jungles and the extremes of human behaviour'. Wars, elections and criminal trials, disasters, victories and games were his assignments. South America, Hollywood and the

Brooklyn Dodgers; Tahiti, the Vatican, the Congo. All over America and the world he flew and drew.

He said he had put himself in many positions, though soon found that few were more advantageous than that of the cartoonist.

# 9

In a country with a small population a reporter with, say, ten years experience feels not only that he or she has interviewed everyone, but interviewed them all at least twice.

In such a country experienced reporters sometimes feel they are carrying the biographies of the entire resident and visiting population around in their brains.

The first time I interviewed Levinson was on his NASA visit to Perth. In his room in the Esplanade Hotel (long since demolished by the developers), gazing across the grassy foreshore to the river, Levinson, an expansive interviewee, confirmed many of my suspicions about cartoonists.

'We get away with murder,' he said cheerily. He and I were both pleased with that quote. His accent required some concentration on my part because his words came out in slices, strata, the American twang overlaying the European, but the flow was enthusiastic and sportive.

'We take liberties right and left. The laughing subversive is allowed leeway,' he said.

I wrote it down.

Who else, he wondered, could wound a dangerous politician and then have the victim beg for the libel to frame on his study wall? The *original* insult, if the defamer could please spare it, the actual drawing, so the slander was raw and rich and personal. And, it had to be said, women seemed to find cartoonists attractive. Of course it was silly, he laughed, but why knock it?

'Is that so?' I wondered. Even then he was balding and bony, all nose and forehead and thick accent, quite unprepossessing. My brash young voice hung in the air, full of disbelief and jealousy.

Actually, he was treating me kindly. He'd ordered beer and chicken sandwiches on room service. He hadn't raised an eyebrow at my youth and inexperience and my dogged list of prepared questions. He seemed to be enjoying himself in this suntanned frank town.

'I have theories. Perhaps they are seen as both funny and courageous,' he said. 'Quite a sexual combination, if so.'

Though I scribbled furiously in my new Pitman's shorthand I couldn't see *The West Australian* running that. I probably frowned. He mused that maybe the satirical quip and the brave barb gave them an iconoclastic aura.

'Add the intrigue of sensitivity and the drama of the artistic temperament and you have a very interesting fellow.'

'Maybe,' I muttered. I couldn't believe this man. Perhaps I put my notebook down and took a long gulp of beer, gazed across the Narrows at a yacht battling the sea breeze.

He abruptly dropped the arch manner. 'But I'm under no illusion that Levinson-the-architect's sex appeal would have held up,' he announced.

It was amazing to him, he said, sitting here in this far-off place, to think that architecture had been his original course. Oh, he felt a paternal sympathy for the

'big-nosed boy' who had enrolled in 1935 in the Politecnico, Facoltà di Architettura, in Pisa—'a small college
much taken with Cubism'. He had been timid, studious,
a foreigner, and his Italian wasn't good.

'I found the study of architecture a wonderful training
for anything but architecture,' he pronounced.

I wrote it down and underlined it.

It was the first time he had drawn from life ('*dal vero*—
from the true') and he thought such truth demanded
the elimination of whatever natural talent he possessed.
'I was always terrified that what I drew might eventually
become a building.' He had drunken student nightmares
of his apartment blocks crumbling, his skyscrapers rent
by fissures, of sheets of plate-glass popping from the
windows of his office buildings and spearing into the
city crowds.

Across the river the ranks of suburban bungalows with
their uniform red and grey tiled roofs shimmered in the
haze of the summer afternoon. I took a draught of beer
and considered the question of architecture for a moment.
In front of the hotel the authorities had poured filling
into the river to make an expressway and a huge carpark.
Seagulls rose and settled on the mud.

'It was traditional for the students to blame the Tower
for such fears,' Levinson said. 'To blame it but to love
it. What a wonderful symbol for the study of architecture!'

It had made Levinson-the-architect uneasy. ('It took
Einstein to face the question of the Tower of Pisa and
legitimise its lean even in the minds of engineering
students,' he told me.) But Levinson-the-maybe-artist had
preferred it that way.

He quoted Einstein at me. Doggedly I wrote it down.
(I could have filled three or four columns already.) Einstein had remarked on the Tower being a beautiful sym-

bol for the fact that human beings couldn't foresee the social implications of their works.

'Don't you agree?' he asked me.

'Yes,' I said. My leaden questions soon brought him down to earth. 'When did you begin cartooning?'

It was in Pisa that he had begun publishing cartoons in the student magazines, poking mild fun at the fascists and getting away with it. Or perhaps his undergraduate satire had arrived at its point by such a roundabout route as to render it inoffensive. Either way, its publication encouraged him to see himself less as an architect and more as a cartoonist.

How and when had he begun to draw? I asked next. When had he developed his famous line?

Oh, he remembered the enthusiastic reception his parents had given his first scribbles, the exclamations of wonder, the colored inks his father brought home from his factory, the yellow art-gum erasers crumbly as cheese, the haberdashery order forms he drew on. They treated him like a genius and kissed his inky fingers, kept his pencils sharpened and pinned his efforts on the pantry door.

'What they didn't know,' he said solemnly. 'What I can still recall vividly here in the Esplanade Hotel in Perth, Western Australia, is that at four I was faking and I knew it.'

What he had been trying to do, but couldn't explain to them, was to write. And nothing simple either. Long screeds about his existence—the story of himself, Mother and Father, their house and little empire of being. He wanted to write about the taste of stewed quinces for tea and the moustached faces they drew on his boiled eggs and the stork's nest on the roof. But, like all children, he was keenly aware of his limitations. He sensed he was virtually illiterate so he tried to bluff it out.

'Bluff and subterfuge are behind everything,' he told me. 'Art. Life.'

I gave him a look.

'Write it down,' he said.

Little Leon had copied the shape and flow of his parents' writing, but immediately realised that this scrawl didn't really say anything. So he made his fake grown-up script encompass pictures of the things—his ginger cat Jimpy, his parents, the swan trademark on a packet of his father's socks—that he was 'writing' about. And his line became his way of writing.

'And today?' I wondered.

As an adult he still saw his line as make-believe script, he said, as a link between imaginative but staccato kiddy drawings and the flowing longhand of maturity. But while he had sought ever since to present his vision of the world through his drawings, he had never quite shaken off the feeling that he was still bluffing it out. The grafting of English on to the vine of his European languages had only compounded his guilt that he was avoiding the issue. Of writing. Perhaps of facing up to adulthood.

'I was stuck with my line,' he told me.

For what it is worth, he still has it today. It is there in his comic crayfish; in his leering, vaguely familiar pirate with the ear-rings and eye patch; in his simple coconut palm—on the chests of tourists and schoolchildren, on the brown bosoms of drink waitresses. It is long, circuitous, very faint in parts, but always continuous.

# 10

On Levinson's visit to Perth for *Life* and NASA in 1962 Spargo proudly took him to see his shipwreck. In the early summer they drove down the coast and Spargo gave him scuba lessons and then dived with him over the remains of the *Fortuyn.*

Levinson was much affected, as Spargo had promised him he would be, by the experience: the beauty, the strange freedom, the complex animal-mineral structures of reefs and cliffs and dunes. He revelled in the exercise, the fresh seafood (especially the crayfish, plucked by Spargo, barehanded, from under the reef ledges in front of him, cooked immediately in an old kerosene tin, and eaten with no adornment or garnish other than fresh bread and vinegar) and, to his surprise, the hot, dry weather. Furiously, he made sketches and notes, on land and—using a new laminated paper developed for marine archeologists and biologists—even underwater.

Then on the last two days of their stay the trailing edge of Cyclone Anna struck the coast, striking hard and unusually far southward. The seas rose and smashed against the reefs. The gale howled through their tent fly. Spargo was disappointed, even apologetic, but Levinson was truly pleased. Now he had the complete picture.

He sat outside in the storm, his peeling nose and burnt forehead into the gritty wind, sketching on his laminated paper while all around him whirled weed scraps and shells and the timeless marine smells of reclaimed jugs and candlesticks and coins and ballast bricks, all swept up in a pungent stinging shrapnel by the tropical wind.

His drawings from this visit would eventually appear in *Life* in two consecutive issues in June 1963. The accompanying text for the shipwreck drawings was chosen with great care. It said

### How to represent a tempest

If you wish to represent a tempest consider and arrange its effects when the wind blowing over the face of the sea and of the land lifts and carries with it everything that is not fixed firmly in the general mass. And in order to represent this tempest you must first show the clouds riven and torn and flying with the wind, together with storms of sand blown up from the sea-shore, and boughs and leaves swept up by the strength and fury of the gale and scattered with other light objects through the air.

Let the sea be wild and tempestuous, and full of foam whirled between the big waves, and the wind should carry the finer spray through the stormy air resembling a dense and all-enveloping mist. The ship should be shown with sails rent and the shreds fluttering in the air in company with the broken ropes and some of the masts split and fallen, and the vessel itself lying disabled and broken by the fury of the waves, with the men shrieking and clinging to the fragments of the wreck.

Make the clouds driven by the impetuous winds, hurled against the cliff tops, and there wreathing and eddying like waves that beat upon rocks; the very air should strike terror through the deep darkness caused by the dust and mist and heavy clouds.

The instructions *How to represent a tempest* were of course those of Leonardo da Vinci and recommended to the *Life* editors by Levinson himself as being nicely apt for the New World. Rather, the *new* New World.

# 11

I had suddenly warmed to Levinson when he revealed to me the origin of his continuous line. His line came back to me as I struggled to make sense of my story.

It occurred to me that investigative reporting, or indeed writing a traditional novel, is also largely a matter of attaining the continuous line, of making the connections, of maintaining the flow of narrative. It's rather like joining the numbers one to two to three and so on in a child's dot-to-dot puzzle and discovering a giraffe.

I realised that it fitted in with my belief in life's ricochet effect. Individual paths follow one another. People and events career off each other only to remain inextricably linked.

My cardinal example of the ricochet principle actually begins with me. A factual story. *Dal vero.*

In 1953, when I was nine, the Lone Avenger wrote to me. 'Dear Bob,' he wrote. (I was never called Bob but for the Lone Avenger I was happy to be Bob.) 'Congratulations! You have won a Lone Avenger gun-belt and holster. Your prize follows by parcel post. Keep up the good work!'

Each month's Lone Avenger comic book featured a find-the-bullet contest. The contest was based firmly on the principle of the ricochet. The back cover would show a scene where, say, the Lone Avenger had just shot the six-gun from the hand of a whiskered gunslinger. (A flash like a spiky flower would blossom where the bullet struck the crook's revolver; a grimace of pain and surprise would pass across his face. 'Aagh!' he would say. Or, if he was foul-mouthed, '*#@+&*X#*!')

You had to work out the angle of deflection, guess the route taken by the victorious bullet and mark with a neat cross (ink, not pencil) where you estimated it was now.

However, what intrigued me as a nine-year-old was how the whole premise of the contest depended on time and motion being abruptly suspended. The presumption had to be made that the Lone Avenger's bullet wasn't buried in the wall of a clapboard feed store or in a tree (or even in a person, some goggling cowboy onlooker) a hundred yards outside the cartoon's frame, but hanging weightless somewhere in the dusty air.

I was almost as pleased by the Lone Avenger's letter, by his easy familiarity (calling me 'Bob'), as I was by the actual prize when it arrived in Perth by surface mail five or six weeks later. A serious child, I was impressed by the solemn turn the letter took at the end: 'Always remember, in victory or defeat, to obey the Lone Avenger's Code.'

His code was strict and all-encompassing. Its ten points insisted we should worship God, venerate the Queen, honour our parents, be polite to adults, respect people of all creeds, be kind to animals, do at least three good deeds each day, study hard, play healthy outdoor sports and obey the law.

The Lone Avenger wanted us to make something of ourselves. This was 1953.

Although Lone Avenger comic books were Australian—illustrated, printed and published in Sydney—their characters and terrain came out of an unspecified country very like the American West.

The Lone Avenger wore a sheriff's star, and his town of saloons, banks and livery stables was familiar to us from the movie matinees and other officially American comics.

Despite the heat in the desert country to which he brought summary justice, the Lone Avenger wore a hood covering his entire head and tucked into his shirt collar. Only the eye-holes were cut out. We never saw him eat or drink or—of course not—kiss. On top of the hood he wore his Stetson. When his hat was knocked off in a fight, or when he was indoors, the hood gave him a pointy-headed look like a Ku Klux Klansman.

It was never clear to me why he was protecting his identity. Occasionally I wondered whether he was hideously scarred or ugly. But at nine I suspended disbelief. I was sure his reasons were sound. And whatever the reasons, the hood was undoubtedly behind his success both as a lawman and a comic strip character.

How can I describe a masked man? Only by his physique. The Lone Avenger was well-built, tall, though not as tall and muscular as his deputy, Bull. Bull had cauliflower ears and a broken nose. Bull was a bit simple and bashful with women. Nevertheless he was a brave and loyal lieutenant, a useful companion in a saloon brawl or canyon shootout.

I remember the Lone Avenger as chivalrous to all women. I am clear about that. He was just as gallant to the ranchers' free-spirited blonde daughters in their checked shirts and boots as he was to the helpless overdressed city ladies who arrived in a tizzy on the noon stage. He was even polite to the sassy dancehall girls. But if he was ever romantically involved he kept it from us.

Strangely, the women didn't seem the least put off by the hood. Indeed, a wistful note usually crept into their thank-yous and goodbyes after he had solved their problems and was about to ride away.

———————

The Lone Avenger was the creation of a young cartoonist named Len Lawson. He signed his name with a proud vertical flourish in every comic strip. So definite and omnipresent was his signature in the cartoon's panels that I came to think of Len Lawson the cartoonist as the Lone Avenger's secret identity. Len Lawson was like Clark Kent to the Lone Avenger's Superman.

I realised it was Len Lawson as well as the Lone Avenger who had written to me.

'Len Lawson' even sounds like the name of a cartoon character. It's a perfect name for the alter ego of an adventure hero. There is a simplicity to it; its alliteration makes it seem imaginary, created by a cartoonist's hand.

Len Lawson had arrived in Sydney from Wagga Wagga, a farming town in south-eastern New South Wales, where his father was a shopkeeper. After working briefly for a printer, the young Lawson trained as a commercial artist and photographer, gradually developing his skills as a cartoonist.

During the late forties and early fifties, before television reached Australia, there was a comic book boom. It coincided with the post-war baby boom. Australia's post-war children grew up reading comics voraciously. All the popular comics were American and though published locally under licence always featured American characters and situations. One or two shrewd local publishers decided to break into this market with indigenous comic books. But they didn't want to break the American spell and alienate a generation of child readers with unfamiliar *Australian* heroes and backgrounds.

So they fostered heroes who were modelled on Americans and who roamed a country called nothing.

————

The Lone Avenger was the leader of the second-hand heroes. The Lone Avenger was making Len Lawson seventy-five pounds a week by the time he was twenty-five in 1953, the year I guessed the angle of ricochet off the trigger-guard of the crook's Colt, then off a boulder, and found the avenging bullet hanging motionless in the air.

At the time he wrote his congraulations to me for tracking the bullet, the male basic wage was fifteen pounds a week. Len Lawson was making something of himself, living well with his wife and three children in the beach suburb of Manly, making a reputation. He was a handsome young fellow, with thick, oiled and combed-back dark hair and a suave Clark Gable moustache. Circumstances, of course, gave him a furtive look when he appeared on the nation's front pages a year later.

*Ricochet.*

————

One morning in May 1954 Len Lawson hired five young photographic models, the oldest twenty-two, the two youngest only fifteen, to pose for a calendar he said he was producing. The assignment was to pose provocatively in 'outdoor' clothing—shorts and swimsuits—in a natural setting.

He drove them to Terrey Hills on the northern outskirts of Sydney. He arranged them in their poses and photographed them against a backdrop of eucalypts and boulders. Then he took a sawn-off .22 rifle, a hunting knife and strips of adhesive plaster from his briefcase and bound and gagged them. He raped two of the models and fondled the others.

Afterwards he was contrite, all apologies. He paid them all their full modelling fees and drove them back to town.

He was arrested immediately, tried and found guilty of two counts of rape. The Lone Avenger of the comic books had become the Terrey Hills Rapist of the afternoon tabloids. Len Lawson was sentenced to death.

————————

A controversy raged about his death sentence. No rapist who had not also committed murder had been executed since the nineteenth century. After several weeks' squabbling the State Government commuted the sentence to life imprisonment.

In prison Len Lawson had to shed the Lone Avenger. The authorities would not let him create his comic books from jail. So he took up a different code. He took religious instruction and became a Catholic. From cartooning he switched to painting, concentrating on biblical images and realistic oil portraits of religious leaders. Perched on a forty-foot ladder he spent months painting murals in the jail chapel: Samson fighting a lion, David and Goliath preparing for battle, Daniel in the lion's den, the Sermon on the Mount, the Crucifixion. Popes Pius

XII and John XXIII filled his canvases. And the local Catholic leaders were not forgotten: he recreated from photographs the stern likeness of Archbishop Daniel Mannix of Melbourne.

This new artistic direction did not escape the authorities' attention. Catholic prison visitors spread the favourable word. Religious sentiment may have affected the nuns' critical faculties but the word got through to the Justice Minister, who was coincidentally a Catholic, coincidentally named Mannix.

Len Lawson, the Terrey Hills Rapist, had been redeemed through love of God and Art. Or at least by a knack for photo-realism.

He was released after serving seven years.

'He was an exemplary prisoner who by his conduct, industry and attitude gained all the remissions to which he was entitled,' announced the Justice Minister.

'He taught murderers to paint and saved them from despair,' carolled the forgiving tabloids.

'I hold no bitterness. I have come out without a chip on my shoulder,' said Len Lawson magnanimously. 'All that is behind me and my paintings are my future.'

He announced that he was presenting his portrait of Archbishop Mannix to the church.

He was now thirty-three. His wife and children had left him. He moved back to the Manly district to start a new life. He painted. He befriended a sixteen-year-old local girl. Their friendship proceeded on a calm, almost lofty plane. She was a quiet girl of whom the tabloids would later deliver their ultimate accolade.

She was 'churchgoing'. 'Churchgoing' was the newspaper euphemism of the day for a virgin.

Two months passed and Len Lawson had made no physical or romantic overtures to her. He was a regular

guest in her parents' home. The past was behind him.
   *Ricochet.*

_____

The Lone Avenger had a complex and imaginative
plan of retribution. It involved the two most glamorous
folk heroines of the day. They were the best known
women in the country, household names, stereotypes,
almost cartoon figures. They were the reigning Miss
Australia (the most beautiful winner in memory) and
the country's most attractive Olympic gold medallist,
known by the press as the 'Golden Girl'.

There was also another young woman who could help
to bring his fantasy to reality—the nun who had
instructed him during his conversion to Catholicism and
who had helped spread the word about his religious
paintings.

'Society' would be forced to hand these three women
over to him. 'Society' would have little choice.

This maelstrom of a scheme had as its vortex his
friendship with the 'churchgoing' sixteen-year-old. Len
Lawson flattered her with an offer to paint her portrait.
Her dark beauty should be captured on canvas. He would
try to do justice to the soul behind her wide eyes.

She came to his flat for the first sitting. When the
'churchgoing' girl repulsed his advances (as he had
expected, wanted, her to do) he bludgeoned her unconscious with a sock filled with sand. He stripped her, trussed
her up and raped her. When she regained consciousness
he strangled her with a piece of rope. Then he took
a hunting knife and stabbed her to death.

After ejaculative frenzy came remorse and decorum.
He replaced the panties on the body. With her eyeliner

pencil he scrawled on her chest, 'God forgive me—Len.' He sat and wrote a letter to his parents in Wagga Wagga. 'I have done a dreadful thing. Whatever this monster is that moves in my body, it did it with a vengeance this time. I can't express the horror I feel at what I've done.'

The Lone Avenger was not remorseful for long. He gathered up an automatic rifle, two hundred rounds of ammunition, a periscope and eighty short lengths of rope and drove one hundred miles into the Southern Highlands to an Anglican girls' boarding school at Moss Vale. The girls were saying their morning prayers when he burst into the school chapel and threatened them with the rifle. He was in command.

He handed the headmistress a message. No one would be hurt if the three women of his fantasy were brought to him: Miss Australia, the Golden Girl and the nun. But the sheer number of girls before him created unexpected hysterical uncertainties. He couldn't trust anyone to leave the room and he couldn't keep his eyes on them all. He waved his rifle and strode about. Time passed. Schoolgirls moaned. Outside, cars passed along the road and magpies sang on the hockey fields. The headmistress managed to write a note for help on her prayer-book marker and drop it from the chapel window.

Police arrived. The Lone Avenger fired wildly, inaccurately, but it was easy to track this bullet. His shot killed a fifteen-year-old schoolgirl. The headmistress grabbed the rifle barrel and the police overpowered him.

At his murder trial Len Lawson refused to claim insanity. 'I am sane and rational,' he declared. 'My conscience will punish me for the rest of my life.'

Capital punishment had been wiped from the statutes. He received another life sentence.

The headmistress received a medal for gallantry.

The portrait of Archbishop Mannix, refused by the church, was passed in at auction without a bid being made.

———————

In maximum security prison there were no painting privileges. However, Len Lawson, this time in prison for life not 'life', his papers stamped Never To Be Released, was again a model prisoner. Eventually he re-entered the mainstream of prison life. He was returned to a 'normal' prison—Parramatta. He helped other prisoners with their hobbies. He built scenery for theatrical performances. He began painting his portraits again.

Ten years passed. Now aged forty-four and a prison veteran, he became president of the Inmates' Association. The association organised prison concerts by outside entertainers with the help of a prisoners' aid charity called the Robin Hood Committee.

(Robin Hood and the Lone Avenger: they were analogous. The hoods, the code of honour, the desire for retribution.)

In June 1972 the two groups sponsored a concert by professional singers, dancers and musicians in the prison chapel. The concert was warmly received by the prisoners and afterwards the entertainers were invited to stay for a cup of tea.

The prettiest member of the concert party was a twenty-three-year-old jazz-ballet dancer. Earlier, while she was dancing for the prisoners one of the men, photographing her for his later erotic perusal, had unavoidably got Len Lawson in the background of his snapshot. In the photograph Lawson is sitting in the front row. On his face is a half-amused, blasé expression. His chin rests on one hand, his legs are crossed.

Over tea and biscuits the jazz-ballet dancer admired one of Lawson's paintings, a portrait of John F. Kennedy.

'It's beautiful. You're very clever,' she said.

'Thank you.'

*Ricochet.*

Minutes later a Robin Hood committee-woman announced that it was time to go.

'Everyone leaves but her,' announced Len Lawson. He held a knife at the throat of the jazz-ballet dancer and another knife at her back.

———————

Two other prisoners and a warder leapt on Lawson and subdued him. The dancer, though cut on the neck and her left hand where she had grabbed at a knife, was more shocked than badly wounded. In the jail hospital five stitches were put in her neck wound, three in her hand. She was taken home, very distressed.

She remained badly disturbed by the attack. She needed psychiatric care and spent months in a private psychiatric hospital. She threatened suicide several times. Her main fear was that Lawson would escape from jail and kill her. She was terrified of strange men and frightened of anyone walking behind her.

Urged on by her psychiatrist, the jazz-ballet dancer sued the New South Wales Government for compensation for the attack on her in one of its prisons. The psychiatrist gave evidence to the Supreme Court that her 'phobic anxiety' had been caused by Lawson's attack.

The psychiatrist was the star witness at the hearing. He was a commanding, even arrogant, personality; a leader in his profession. His career had begun in 1950 when psychiatry was considered the last frontier of medicine. His speciality was psychosurgery.

The psychiatrist had the disconcerting professional habit of imparting to his new patients the information that the world was divided into two types of people: Martians and Earthlings.

'Martians can tell who each other are, but Earthlings, alas, can't tell who the Martians are,' he would say. Martians appreciated the finer things in life whereas the mediocre Earthlings were content with the fundamentals. 'The only way one can be happy,' the psychiatrist explained, 'is to fulfil one's predetermined Martian goals—to use one's brains and keep striving.' The psychiatrist left his patients in no doubt as to which planet *he* came from.

The psychiatrist told the Supreme Court that his patient the jazz-ballet dancer was now a hopelessly depressed person who would need to spend most of her life in psychiatric hospitals.

The judge said he was satisfied there was a connection between her mental condition and the attack at the jail. He rejected the government's claim that her phobic anxiety was the result of an unhappy love affair.

She was awarded a large sum in compensation.

---

*Ricochet.*
Nineteen months after being awarded the compensation money the jazz-ballet dancer was found dead.

Police and ambulancemen called to her flat found her body lying on the living-room floor. She appeared to have died from an overdose of sleeping pills. At her funeral her family received a letter informing them that the psychiatrist was the executor and sole beneficiary of her will.

The psychiatrist maintained at her inquest that he had stopped treating her six months before her death, when she had seemed 'well', but that he had 'kept in touch' with her.

The coroner returned a finding that she had died from a self-administered overdose of barbiturates. However, her family complained that they were not satisfied with the decision. They petitioned the Attorney-General that they had 'new evidence' to present.

Her sister told the press: 'Her death came as a great shock because she was on the road to mental recovery. She had found a good job and was really improving.'

A new inquest was called. The family and friends of the jazz-ballet dancer gave evidence that she and the psychiatrist had been having an affair. He had begun the romance shortly after he started treating her. She had had an abortion in July, 1977. The child would have been born about the date she killed herself.

*Ricochet.*

———————

The second inquest attracted wide publicity. The psychiatrist denied the allegations of the affair, and of having made her pregnant. Though the second coroner came to the same finding—that the jazz-ballet dancer had died from self-administered barbiturates—the new inquest focussed public and peer group attention on the treatment methods of her psychiatrist.

He was a leading advocate of a treatment known as continuous narcosis, or deep sedation therapy. He would admit his depressed patients to a particular private hospital on Sydney's North Shore where they were given heavy doses of barbiturates and rendered unconscious for ten or twelve days at a time. While they were comatose the patients would be given shock treatment.

Cases came to light of patients having died while

undergoing his deep sedation therapy. Relatively young and physically healthy patients had died from coronary occlusions and pneumonia. Former patients came forward claiming to have been permanently mentally and physically harmed by the treatment.

A citizens' committee and a member of parliament began accumulating a mass of material on the psychiatrist and his controversial methods. They gathered documentation alleging at least sixteen deaths and thirty-five cases of mental and physical impairment, which in several cases, including that of the jazz-ballet dancer, had led to suicide.

Former patients and their families began legal actions for compensation against the psychiatrist. The government and the Medical Board announced inquiries into his methods and professional competence. The day he was due to face the first of the malpractice suits his body was found in his car north of Sydney.

*Ricochet.*

He had taken an overdose of the barbiturate Tuinal, the same drug he had prescribed for his patients. He had washed the pills down with Heineken.

His suicide note had a final Martian touch. 'I'd rather be having a Scotch but this bottle of imported beer will have to do.'

---

Was this the end of the bullet's momentum at last? Could I now presume, having charted the angles of deflection, guessed the trajectory, that the Lone Avenger's bullet, having ricocheted off the five photographic models and the 'churchgoing' sixteen-year-old and the fifteen-year-old boarding-school girl and the jazz-ballet dancer and her aborted child and finally the psychiatrist, was now hanging, weightless, in the humid air over the dead psychiatrist's BMW on a dirt road off Sydney's northern expressway?

The psychiatrist? Should the arrogant, manipulative and unethical psychiatrist also be charted as a victim of the ricochet? Indeed, yes. I was shown copies of pertinent hospital records and nursing files. Certain facts have since come to light. Relationships are rarely one-sided; relationships are more, and less, than they seem.

Could it be that the psychiatrist's emotions had also been powerfully wrought by his exploitative affair with his patient, the young and attractive jazz-ballet dancer? Could it be that he felt acute guilt when she killed herself? (And then left him all her compensation money?) Could it be that such a man, married, a leader in his profession, such a *Martian*, suffered not only great professional embarrassment at the allegations of their love affair, but even greater personal embarrassment at being forced to produce before the second inquest medical proof that he had not fathered her aborted child because his sperm count was negative and that he was sterile?

Journalism is chary of such questions. Journalism falls back on documents and records. The records show the psychiatrist was himself treated for clinical depression one month after her death. He was suicidal. He admitted himself to the same private hospital and was given a course of his own deep sedation therapy—an act of faith if ever there was one.

So could I now mark with a neat inked cross where the bullet had finally stopped? Where time and motion were abruptly suspended, over a parked BMW on a dirt road?

Not entirely.

The bullet never stops. Worse, it fragments. Splinters

fly everywhere. Each shard begins its own flight and the process continues.

My copy of the private hospital admission files of the psychiatrist's patients from 30 November, 1969 to 15 April, 1980 lists 1,217 names. The list is impressive, if only as a weathercock, a straw in the wind of the times.

Among the patients who underwent deep sedation therapy (with associated electro-convulsive treatment) for depression—between 8.15 a.m. on 11 March and 4.30 p.m. on 21 March, 1979—was a Caroline Jane Castle (born 28.3.38), address care of the Sheraton Wentworth Hotel, Sydney. Next of kin: Fiona Castle (daughter), address care of the Sheraton Wentworth (room 912).

## 12

Levinson was a guest at the Castles' party because of his space connection.

Spargo was invited because he had found sunken treasure.

Space and treasure: in 1962 they had captured the West Australian imagination. That summer night, marshalling his guests out on to the terrace overlooking the river, Peter Castle could easily believe that space might equal treasure.

I am drawing on memory now, personal experience, provincial newsroom orthodoxy.

After John Glenn's orbital flight, and his public acknowledgement of the glow from below, I remember Perth basking in its image as The City of Light.

The City of Light began as a sub-editor's heading in *The West Australian*. At once it was picked up by the wire-services and then the American press. The local businessmen agreed that you couldn't *pay* for that sort of PR. *The City of Light* would finally put Perth on the map. American investment? Things looked very rosy.

Already the Americans had invited the Lord Mayor to take part in New York's tickertape parade for the space hero. No one told the Americans that the mayor had

actually opposed the suggestion to turn on the lights
and had fought it bitterly in the city council. The mayor
certainly didn't tell them it had been the brainwave of
a shrewd reporter, to beef up the news on his town hall
beat.

The Lord Mayor of Perth, Western Australia, had his
own open limousine in the parade and no astronaut was
more overwhelmed by the emotion of the occasion, or
waved and smiled more heartily at the cheering New
Yorkers.

As his city had beamed up at gallant John Glenn,
so he beamed up at the towers of Wall Street.

Peter Castle, too, liked the look and sound of *The
City of Light* and said so at the time in a press roundup
of comments from prominent citizens. Some of the more
excitable businessmen even advocated changing Perth's
name to The City of Light. Castle drew the line at this.
But, somewhere else?

Then the American vice-consul informed the local
press that the National Aeronautics and Space Admin-
istration would be pleased to send over its official artist
to be inspired by The City of Light for *Life* magazine.

Castle acted quickly. Within an hour of reading this
item he had set up the reception for the *Life* man. The
guest list? Wasn't there an astronaut in town again?
Gordon Cooper? Deke Slayton? The vice-consul of
course. The Lord Mayor—try leaving him out of it! The
usual business leaders. And who better to inspire the
man from *Life* than their own explorer and man-of-the-
moment, Don Spargo?

Spargo was a celebrity not just because he had finally
found his treasure but because he had been vindicated,
because he had persevered and prevailed. His success
brought out the sentimentality in people—in the Castles'
wealthy set as much as anywhere.

In December 1962 Peter Castle could not have been more pleased that Spargo had finally become lucky. The manner in which he was seen to take him up that summer: the weekend all-male fishing trips on the *Spindrift*, the race meetings and the parties of course, indicated that he found him refreshing company. Spargo was his sort of man: earthy, reckless and unaffected.

However, this mentorial attitude alone, so obvious to anyone who observed Perth's small power structure in those days, wouldn't necessarily have made him engineer Spargo's turf club membership much less parade him before local society with the man from *Life* and NASA.

Two days after Spargo's discovery Castle had become his partner in a syndicate to recover the treasure. It was his legal firm which arranged for the wreck to be declared and registered with the Receiver of Wrecks and the Dutch consulate.

But it was not a share of the treasure which attracted Castle to back Spargo's recovery efforts. He maintained in the papers that it was the sport of the thing. The publicity opportunities were obvious to everyone. There was also the option he held on two thousand acres of coastal sand dunes and gravelly scrub in the vicinity of the wreck.

These were heady innocent days, when astronauts and NASA men came to your parties and sent flowers to your wife next day; broke hearts and drank like fish; came fishing for kingies and jewies like one of the boys; sucked crayfish legs and bought champagne at the Latin Quarter; charmed everything that moved with their lazy accents and crewcuts.

Opportunities seemed limitless. Man was soaring up into space and diving down into the sea. And for once these exciting events were converging right here, at the forgotten end of the world. Perth was at the centre of things. Between the cosmos and the bottom of the sea there was land and Castle had the option on it.

He was in a wonderful position. He could choose whether it would be space or treasure which held the secret to the city he would create out of the sandhills.

# 13

By the time I was trying to gather Spargo's story together twenty years later, tracking back and forth across the country in search of court transcripts, affadavits, old interviews, new interviews, fragments and recollections right across the board, there was not much heady innocence left, in Perth or elsewhere.

The opportunities had had definite limits.

That summer of 1983–84 there was a record-breaking heatwave in Western Australia. Spargo remarked on it to both Rosanna and Butterworth on the last day of the trial.

I have an impression of him in his clammy cell in the east. Journalism might disregard it because it flows over into imagination and subjectivity. However, it has its logic.

I see him in the memories of his girlfriend and his lawyer. He is sitting on the bunk in his one-man cell in the metropolitan remand centre of Long Bay jail trying not to think of the next day, concentrating instead on the torrid peculiarities on the other side of the continent.

Back home, if he could believe the papers, the absence of the Doctor was on everyone's lips.

During the five weeks of the trial he had picked up

occasional strange paragraphs from the Sydney newspapers, and on her visits and during court recesses
Rosanna had once or twice supplied details from the
previous evening's TV news. Of course he was too pre-
occupied to take much notice. But then that afternoon,
after the jury had finally retired, with nothing more that
he or Rosanna or Butterworth could do, Butterworth
had given him a stack of hometown papers to take back
to jail.

'Something to take your mind off tomorrow,' he said.

To an extent the lawyer was right. The image of the
dogs hanging themselves would implant itself in
anyone's mind.

After January had passed without the Doctor—the sea
breeze—arriving, Perth's dogs had apparently begun
strangling themselves on their leads. The papers didn't
mention any numbers but there were enough victims
for the Royal Society for the Prevention of Cruelty to
Animals to be 'most alarmed' at the trend. Tethered
animals, fierce northern European guard dogs, protectors
of the rich, were hanging themselves all over town.

Spargo saw them straining to escape not just the relentless heat but the whole country, indeed the hemisphere.

By the second week in February the Doctor's non-
arrival seemed to be the biggest news story of the western
summer. It was bigger than the discovery of further
valuable diamond deposits in the north and increasingly
adventurous business takeovers in the city.

It was certainly treated as a bigger story, even as the
trial neared its end, than the Queen versus Donald Patrick
Spargo and Rosanna Marie McMahon.

He could see the trial had made only the middle or
back news pages each day. On some days there was no
coverage at all. Once again he felt slighted. His was a
bigger story than suiciding dogs, even if they did stick

in the mind. The papers had their ways of getting even.

There was another sort of press animosity that was almost flattering: when the papers ran the most negative photographs available—those tousled arriving-at-court pictures, furtive flanked-by-cops pictures—and led their court coverage always with the prosecution evidence. But by burying the trial under the weather data they were implying something else—that he was and had always been of only minimal interest. That he was page fifteen news.

Meanwhile, they (and I know he thought of them as *they*) were comprehensively listing all the agricultural mishaps, stock losses, freak accidents and extreme incidents caused by the weather. It seemed to him there was an odd possessive pride in the newspapers' accumulation of such adverse statistics. Hottest ever. Longest ever. Driest ever. Records tumbled as in the Olympics.

He smiled wryly. He had to admit they knew their market. They knew how their readership thought. The readers were proud of all these misadventures. These people had a communal inferiority complex. They pined for any recognition in the big outside world. Records were records, and wouldn't these stun those self-centred eastern staters!

He leaned back on his bunk, the headlines swimming before his eyes. When he closed them extraordinary hot vistas opened before him. Grapes cooked on the vine, potatoes in the dusty soil. Dobermans and German Shepherds hanged themselves. Schools closed down. People had to wrap themselves in wet towels in order to sleep at night, and prowlers, taking advantage of the doors and windows so despairingly thrown open to catch any cool draught (and the well-reported disappearance of watch dogs), freely contemplated crimes against property and person.

What the papers were doing was distancing themselves and his hometown from him. They were re-defining what would become the conventional local wisdom about him and permitting people to rearrange the past.

———————

I see him in the broken mirror of his own memory, trying to put it back together from so many shattered pieces:

*Waking and you're still there. The famous body and pyjama smell seeping through the house. Coming back even now to haunt me. Here I am clinging like a baby to your legs, face against the famous pyjama smell. OK, I'll watch you shave. I like to. I'm here dozy on the cold bath edge. Friendly lemon light coming through the louvres. In the doorway Mother's weepy smile bringing the hot water jug. Vague toasty smells on her. Gown and nightie noises slide away down the hall and it's just us. Shave away there. Brush on the lather. Scrape the chin. Let the soap and pyjama smell fill the room. Listen to me chatter. Watch me with your eyes in the mirror—I can do clever things. Yes, dab a jolly blob of lather on my nose! Yes, I'll have a jaunty pilot's moustache too. Careful with your own mo. Don't slice it off. Blow out your cheek like that again. And the top lip. Make the funny daddy stretching neck. Why not hum a bit. Whistle through your teeth. Peaches and cream. Bye-bye blackbird. Slosh and razor away for ever.*

*But there goes the flannel over the cheeks. Into the ears and eyes. Removing the soapy mask. Are those new holes in your face? (Jungle sores? Bullet scars?) It's a thinner face. A strangely yesterday's out-of-date face. A mirrored face. Oh the swiftly vanishing luxury of your two faces filling the house instead of none. The blurry familiarity and baggy twinkling eye power. But here comes the assurance of the hair tonic in the palm. Purposeful hand-rubbing. Debonair tortoise-shell comb shrewdly flicks out from nowhere into the glistening hair. Please stop the confidence and brisk movements. I wish . . . Keep the pyjama smell. The soapy daddy cheek smell. Stay the ruffled sleeper and smiling slow mover. The Saturday underarm bowler. The gentle weekend drop-kicker. No. My throat clenches at the inevitable sweet gagging smell of the hair tonic. Inevitable. OK. Shirt. Tie. Polish. Newly-ironed uniform smell. OK. Bye. Gone. Eat my Weeties. Jolly Willie Weeties still carrying a packet of Weeties on which jolly Willie Weeties carries a packet of Weeties . . . Willie, smaller and smaller, marching on into infinity.*

*In the wash basin one thousand tiny hair specks clinging. Outlasting. And your smell. Treacherously spit my Colgate on your last traces.*

# 14

See it through Spargo's eyes.

Some notes that pertain to his condition in April 1983 (recorded by P.J. O'Halloran of Baker and Wallsend in the visitors' room, Long Bay, on his return, in custody, from the Northern Territory):

[*Tone*—defensive and reckless. *Appearance*—Vigorous and energetic. Considering the circumstances, strangely optimistic. Almost devil-may-care. *Adrenalin high? Out of touch with reality?*]

'I've got no excuses. Put it down to adventure. *Qui cherche trouve.* What did I have to lose? I've pulled some things off, you know, in my time. Found a ship or two. Questioned history. Changed the nation's laws. Got into the archives.

...You seem to be harping on me jumping bail. Listen, I just went missing on a charge with no validity anyway. The money was too good. I've got legal cases to fight, you know. I needed the money.

...But it wasn't that. The idea appealed to me. It smelled of high adventure. Sounded like there was no risk. A chance to bore it up the stupid government. Actually it was the perfect movie getaway, arranging with my partners to leave some clothes et cetera with them so I could vanish properly. Looking like I'd been abducted. Left with no money on me deliberately. Intrigue? Of course I loved the intrigue.

...It was a story by itself. These two ex-Vietnam blokes approached me to do a job. They had information about some big weaponry bases abandoned by the Yanks after World War II. I was offered a hundred grand to go up north and pick up a truckload of weapons. They'd sell them to gun shops, collectors, Pacific resistance movements.

...They laid on heavy hints. CIA contacts, that sort of thing. Who knows? Who recognises bulldust these days? It was important that these were *old* weapons though, .303s not SLRs. Not traceable.

...I found the weapon dumps sitting like pyramids in the desert. A cinch to get inside. But then the gas! Toxic. Seems as if the Yanks intended using gas if the Japs invaded Australia. No-one knew, didn't tell us or anything, kept it as a last resort. The dumps were full of it. The metal canisters had corroded and the gas was leaking everywhere. Well I was weeping, vomiting, hae-morrhages in the eye veins, nosebleeds. And no birds or lizards, no bloody bull-ants for fifty yards in any direction. Same situation in the Kimberley dump, same deal in the Gulf and northern Queensland. Everywhere I went this bloody gas like the Pharoah's curse.

...Drove the empty truck five hundred miles with one good eye. Met up with my contacts at Alice Springs as arranged. I walked into the bar at the Travelodge covered in blood and dust. I've got snot and goo down my pants, the dud eye's still projecting tears and they're drinking by the pool wearing sunglasses and white shoes. Jesus, they say, what's this? I say, kaput. And I need some money anyway. I've put a few things at risk here, doing your dirty work. I'm a bail absconder. I've breathed toxic substances. That's blood on my shirt from your clever scheme. Cop these eyes.

...They start off angry but I look so bad they calm down. We'll think about it, they say. Then the serious drinking starts at the Travelodge. Them Chivas Regal, Napoleon brandy. Me sticking to beer on purpose. Mad of them to drink spirits in the outback, still snoring like road-trains at six next morning. No choice but to put the DO NOT DISTURB sign on their doors, disable the truck, take their wallets and guns and head north in their Land-Rover, thinking they won't dare tell the police. Yes, I was wrong...'

O'Halloran, the solicitor who took these notes at Long Bay, was sacked by Spargo even before the committal hearing began. Spargo was swapping lawyers almost weekly at this stage. It would take him a week to brief them on the case and they would just begin to have the chronology right and he would dismiss them or they would resign.

Without exception they were glad to be out of it, even those lawyers who had been willing to tempt fate on this case on the understanding they would represent him in some of the complex constitutional battles he was still fighting elsewhere. It was difficult for an outsider, an easterner, to get to the essence of Spargo by then. What came across was the recklessness, the tawdry fool-hardiness, rather than the obsession and deep disillusion. Hectic fatalism was beyond most comprehension. The only way to understand him was to go back and start again.

# 15

There was no conventional newspaper wisdom on Spargo between 1957 and late 1962. The few reporters and photographers who had had their fingers burnt the first time were jaundiced and believed him capable of anything. Others liked him, sympathised and overlooked the irregularities.

There was general agreement, however, that until the moment he surfaced with the coral-encrusted elephant tusk his status, at best, was Local Character. He was someone who had found a treasure and then lost it; literally a loser. He existed as a phone number in reporters' address books, listed not under his name but under Shipwrecks or Spearfishing or Sharks.

In those doldrum years he was regarded as someone who liked to get his name in the papers. He was a good sport on slow news days and so disdained for it. A sperm whale beached on the south coast? Spargo would be on TV that night, his rubber-suited torso filling the screen, waving off blowflies as he described aberrant migration patterns. Sharks sighted off a popular swimming spot? A Spargo quotation in the evening paper warning swimmers of 'man-eaters' would round off the usual ten panicky paragraphs.

His transformation from character to celebrity caused people to recall the more flamboyant and attractive things he had done, or was said to have done.

An old photograph which surfaced at this time was a vital element in his transformation into reckless adventurer. It showed a thin teenage face grinning inside a diver's helmet. A canvas-clad arm raised a celebratory schooner of beer.

The *Sunday Times* feature story which resuscitated the photograph said that at fourteen, in 1944, Don Spargo was already a hero. Working in his family's marine salvage business and bursting to get into the Japanese war which had killed his father four years before, young Donald had loaded the hull of a bombed East Indian freighter with one hundred pounds of plastic explosive and cleared Wyndham harbour.

We read that in 1944 he made quite a splash. Strange fish bodies floated to the surface for days. Gropers. Stingrays. The piles of the jetty three hundred yards away shifted four inches. After the explosion this cocky teenager plodded into town, into the pub, in full diver's gear, and demanded a beer. A man's drink after a man's job.

In Australia it isn't often that the facts match the yarns. It's photographs which turn the tall stories into facts and legends usually avoid being photographed. Young Spargo was snapped in a diver's helmet and suit holding a glass of beer in a celebratory manner. Satisfactory events involving this equipment and preceding his posing for the camera are thus assumed to have happened.

Legends aren't unduly concerned with inconsistencies. The hotel was a mile from the wharf. No one dressed in lead-weighted boots, bell-helmet, breast plate and canvas suit could have shambled more than a few feet, much less stomped all the way into town like Frankenstein's monster. And he was just fourteen.

It's hard to drink beer in a diver's helmet.

He did admit to me in 1964 that on the afternoon of the harbour clearance twenty years before he'd actually ridden into town as usual after work with the diver's tender, a man too old for the war, in the fellow's Vauxhall van. Two hours later, drunk for the first time on draught beer, he'd been 'urged by the bar' back into the diver's suit for photographs. One had reached the press down south.

'Did you really bomb the freighter?' I asked him at the Palace Hotel. 'Clear the harbour?' Plastic explosive was illegal during the war.

'I badly wanted a war,' he said. 'I was older than my years.'

This was how Caroline Castle perceived him, he thought, at least emotionally. (Physically, he was much younger than she was used to.) He guessed that she needed a mentor figure, someone who straddled the national traditions, someone to get her back to basics.

'Maybe I have a touch of the nineteenth century,' he said. He looked self-conscious but not unhappy with the idea of himself as a buccaneer or bushranger. He had an elbow on the bar and a drink in his hand. His collar and tie for court made his neck swell and the suit jacket was tight at the biceps and shoulders. His prominent eyes and the flush in his cheeks indicated both vigor and disorder, and his free hand worried a drink coaster into paper pellets. 'All this is off the record,' he said. Outside, steam rose from the road. He cleared his throat. 'She always has tears in her eyes,' he said.

Long after the evening of the Castles' party he was still bemused enough to be casting around for reasons.

# 16

As the old social columns attest, until the middle of 1966 Caroline Castle liked to travel and she liked to give parties. In 1966 she came to like travel and parties less and less and by December it was hard to get her to socialise or even move outside the serene suburban rectangle bounded on three sides by the Swan River and on the fourth by Stirling Highway.

I have Leon Levinson's and Spargo's account of the importance she gave at least one party, her own, the cocktail party for Levinson in December 1962 which each man also recognised as a watershed in his life.

I also have Levinson's version of another watershed party: Kermode's party in San Francisco in 1977. His recall was vivid. It seemed he liked parties of all kinds, for the same reason he loved to arrive in a new town and face new situations.

'A party is a small foreign place—and one where the natives are usually friendly,' he told me.

In New York he was asked to many parties because of his job. Cartoonists were acceptable currency anywhere. (He was also single and heterosexual.) He liked the look of cocktail parties, the configuration of so many concentrated and variously shaped bodies under social pressure. He liked the *outline* of cocktail parties. And he didn't mind making up the numbers at dinner parties either. He enjoyed the amusing tension, the vague air of anticipation hanging over the hostess's end of the table. Would he and the spare woman hit it off?

He told me that Linda said he 'twinkled' at parties. She didn't realise that if ever he had twinkled it was the night of Kermode's party.

Daniel Kermode had thrown open his house in fraternal aid of a beleagured Nicaraguan film director. To Levinson, looking back, the evening itself was like the opening scene from a film—though not one of Kermode's (or the Nicaraguan's). It was like a scene from a 'mature' love story, one with a French or Italian director, shot in European autumnal tones, yet with a foreigner's reverence for Americana.

The title could be *The Meeting.* The sun is setting in the Pacific, its waning rays glancing off the strands of the Golden Gate Bridge. In the half-light a Victorian house, eggshell blue, all verticality and steepness, rises out of the Pacific Heights hillside.

Thin mist seeps up the hill from Cow Hollow. A man gets out of a cab and climbs the steps to the house. The small windows opening on to the front porch are mosaics of multi-coloured glass filtering the light from the foyer. Amber, green and red patches dapple the faces and shoulders of the guests arriving on the doorstep.

The visitor is middle-aged, 'ordinary' looking, slightly more rumpled and casually dressed than the other guests around his age, although considerably less casual than those younger than he, most of whom, though American, are dressed like their impressions of Nicaraguan film directors. Several people, casting their eyes around for faces with ever-increasing status, focus on him, attempt briefly to place him and turn away.

The chatter is loud and full of the bravado of tyros. A waiter serves him champagne. As at a gallery opening, the visitor moves slowly through the house sipping champagne and browsing over the director's possessions—the paintings, fussy ornaments and cute bric-a-brac financed by movies celebrating Mafia machismo and the violent vengeance of rogue policemen.

Here are some eighteenth century English bucolic prints, there a china cabinet of Edwardian children's bunny plates. A big fish-tank of butterfly cod. A 1950s jukebox. A framed cheque for one million dollars signed by a famous producer. On one wall is a display of Miros and Chagalls, on another a silk screen of 'Hollywood' signs and a painted tin tray from the 1939 New York World's Fair.

Sauntering with his drink, the visitor takes in all these things, allowing himself to be drawn gradually by the decorative force of his host's personality into the core of the house. Black and white photographs along the way show Kermode with Orson Welles, Hitchcock, Olivier, Brando, Truffaut and Bertolucci; by the time the visitor enters the den he feels well instructed by these pictured associations as to the director's professional standing. Still, he is not prepared for the dramatic show of the three Oscars on the mantel, gleaming icons under their spotlight.

It is like peering into a diorama: *The Film Director's Study*. Everything is perfect. The Oscar statuettes. The clapperboard from *Citizen Kane* over the fireplace. The honorary doctorates in display cases. The framed pages from *Variety*. The envelopes, also framed, announcing his Academy Awards. The walls of alphabetically arranged books. And on a settee among the cedar panels and leather furniture and marble and brass knick-knacks, the wordly souvenirs, the tan, black and beige shades of masculinity and success, sits a small pale woman dressed in red.

He walks over, she rises smiling, they introduce themselves.

'Silver?' he says.

# 17

Linda Silver, that most American of names—peppy, snappy, a perfect fit for headlines. (How right he was there!) At the time it seemed to him the name of a sportswoman. An Olympic swimmer's name. A tennis player's. Or perhaps a TV newsreader's. (Even after thirty years the Americanness of some things fascinated him: faces, jobs, food.)

Then again it could be a comic strip character's name—Brenda Starr, Lois Lane, Linda Silver. She could be a character in one of those realistically drawn romantic comic strips like *The Heart of Juliet Jones*. She was small, blonde and pretty, with a level gaze as she shook hands. Her manner was self-confident yet she remained unobtrusive. She didn't even sound American. The disjunction of her name and appearance and voice struck him the moment they met, in the beam of the spotlight playing on the director's Oscars. Her hand was cool and surprisingly hard in his.

'Silver?' he queried again, on their way downstairs to the screening of the Sandinista documentary. What he was actually saying was: You're not telling me you're Jewish? Even Californian Jewish?

'I kept my ex-husband's name,' she said.

Levinson hoped he detected in the word 'ex-husband' a tentative statement of availability.

Her hand was light on his arm, though very assured, as if she were guiding him past Kermode's movie frippery—the Coke and popcorn machines and old Western posters—and into the serious confines of the cinema. They were there to be educated, her hand said, and to show fraternal support with their cheque books for the beleagured Nicaraguan film director.

'Are you English?' he asked further.

'Originally. I'm American now.'

He raised an eyebrow at her next response. Of all the people Linda did not look like, she did not resemble the general impression of a private investigator.

'Seriously?' he said. She returned a steady glance. Obviously his was the usual reaction. After the Sandinista documentary, wanting to prolong the evening, he suggested coffee and a cognac. She drove them in her battered Thunderbird to the Tosca on Columbus Avenue. The Tosca had a jukebox which played only opera. Pavarotti sang richly and relentlessly from *La Traviata* and they had to shout to make themselves heard above him.

'How did you get into that line of work?' Levinson yelled. He found it hard to smile and shout simultaneously. And when Pavarotti drew breath the espresso machine hissed and bubbled and everyone else in the coffee bar snatched the opportunity to talk. It was bedlam.

The opera was enlarging everyone's gestures. She waved her arms. 'Politics!' she shouted. 'Romance! Literature!' Her teeth were big and white when she smiled and her mouth looked soft and witty. 'They all came together.'

When the record came to an end the relative silence was almost intimate. There was a feeling they shouldn't waste this valuable moment. To overcome the background talk and crockery clatter and hissing espresso machine they leaned closer together, sipped their drinks and communicated urgently in sharp bursts of information and revelation.

She explained that she had been an investigative reporter for a muck-raking anti-establishment magazine in San Francisco. In the course of researching an article, she had interviewed a private investigator on his various operations.

'Until then my image of private eyes was the same as most people's. Seedy types who kicked in motel doors and photographed illicit lovers.' But this man had done undercover work, worked on murder cases and indulged in subterfuge, just like in the films and novels. 'It fulfilled my romantic and literary expectations. It was real Dashiell Hammett stuff and it sounded marvellous.'

The man was leaving his agency so she had applied for his job.

'And you got it, just like that?'

'I had to demonstrate my suitability.'

'At what?' asked Levinson. 'Disguise? Stealth? You don't have a crafty look.'

'Thanks, that's the whole point. I had to prove I was adept at perpetrating what the modern private investigator refers to as the "honest con".'

'Crafty without the crafty look?'

'A bit more than that. I define the "honest con" as the ability to deceive in quest of the truth.'

Pavarotti started up again. The room trembled from the chair legs to the ceiling.

'You give it a moral ring. The shamus business.'

'I was lucky to happen on a job where I had some innate skills.'

He smiled over his brandy glass. 'So you're naturally deceitful?'

She returned a half-smile which indicated that flirting was amusing enough but that she took her life seriously. She listed what she said were her skills, counting them off on her fingers: she had a good knowledge of the law, she was well-educated and she was self-confident. She was forced to lean so close over the table that he could smell her breath. It was clear and fruity, like apples.

'But my main attribute is this. I can walk into a room, into an unpredictable situation, and in a second assess the person I'm dealing with and fit my persona to their expectations.'

She was correct about the self-confidence, he thought.

'Take a look at me,' she went on. 'I'm totally unthreatening. Whomever I'm talking to will take me into their confidence.'.

'Not necessarily.' He laughed. 'Confidentially, how have you fitted your persona to *my* expectations?'

'By telling you the truth.'

'So it all comes down to the truth after all?'

She finished her coffee and put the cup down. She looked him in the eye and rapped him lightly on the knuckles with her coffee spoon.

'Believe me, it's an art. It *is* art. The private investigator exemplifies the same genius for lying and adoration for the truth as the poet.'

Obviously she had turned that phrase before, Levinson thought. He wondered how she knew he had any expectations of either female private eyes or artists.

'Top of the class,' he said.

She drove him back to the St. Francis. He was in town for a small exhibition of his early drawings at the de Young Museum. She wouldn't come up for a drink. Nor would she invite him home for a drink, the drink in inverted commas, the drink that meant bed. She wouldn't even tell him her address.

'Don't be offended,' she said. She explained that she kept her home address secret, her home phone number unlisted. Even the Thunderbird was registered to her office address. She couldn't be traced through the voting lists. She told him all these precautions were necessary safeguards, apologised, gave him a friendly kiss good-night and her office phone number.

She didn't mention at that stage that she also slept with a 9mm Smith and Wesson on her bedside table. She didn't say that when away on assignment she lined drinking glasses along the hotel window-sill as an alarm system just to get a night's sleep.

She didn't indicate the full extent of her seriousness.

And he clambered oafishly out of the car feeling like a thwarted adolescent, waggishly waving his chequebook (where she had written her office phone number) and wondered how 'ex' was the ex-husband.

Opera was still in his ears, brave Latino peasant defiance in his mind's eye, champagne and cognac in his empty stomach. Passion was running high, and ado-ration for the truth. As she accelerated away he heard his voice, too loud, shouting, 'Silver?'

## 18

In 1979 Levinson would have many nights to ponder the name Silver and its relationship with America's cutting edge. Among other things, he would learn (even from the man's own ironic, comradely and equally drunken mouth) about Dr George Silver, supplier of Linda's name.

In his complete exhaustion he would even welcome this new perspective on her: the old life with George. He would learn, drinking with him at night in their unlikely redwood Marin County hideaway (Paul finally fallen asleep at their feet on the living-room floor), that George had been one of Attlee's bright young Jewish grammar school boys, one of the generation which had broken through the English class-education barrier; that, full of lower middle-class gratitude and a relentless ambition, he'd gone on to Oxford from a red-brick university and an adolescence spent in study; even that—when they had met at Oxford five years later—Linda had mocked his donnish Anglo-Saxon camouflage of corduroy, tweed and meerschaum pipes.

Buckeye and laurel branches scraped along the roof. Things rustled and coughed in the woods—deer, raccoons, people perhaps. George and he drank Napa Valley red and started at the beginning, Linda's Smith and Wesson never out of reach.

George had been eight years older than she, already a science graduate with honours in molecular biology, and nearly through his Ph.D. By the time she had her law degree in 1964 George could wait no longer. He accepted the first American scholarship which offered suitable post-doctoral research—from the University of Chicago's department of protein chemistry—and suggested marriage.

According to George, the suggestion had caused Linda some anguish in the beginning. Her vision of America, one of brutality and glamor, was almost overwhelming. 'John Kennedy's assassination was fresh in her mind. Suddenly she envisioned her life among the ghettoes and freedom riders and redneck sheriffs she read about in the *Guardian*. Her only experience of Americans had been negative. She was in a state.'

During her childhood the Americans had built an air base in the fields outside the neighbouring Oxfordshire village of Upper Heyford. Apart from speeding along the village lanes in their convertibles the Americans rarely mixed with the villagers, preferring to keep to their PX store and base school and golf driving range and baseball diamond which lay on former fields of barley and corn and wheat and pasture which had rotated serenely for centuries.

One of those speeding Chevrolet convertibles had knocked Linda's family's odd-job man, old Albert Barker, off his bicycle and killed him. But even this act of gross negligence, treated with the utmost leniency by the English authorities (Albert's age and drinking habits had contributed to the accident, ruled the Oxford coroner), paled in her mind beside another incident involving an American convertible.

Levinson knew most of these pre-George stories by heart, but he filled George's glass and let him proceed. George needed to talk more than he did; George was somehow assuming responsibility for much of what had happened recently. George launched into the story while Levinson sipped his wine and recalled the tale, a jump ahead, his eyes wandering now and then to the gun.

It was a sunny Saturday afternoon. Linda was playing in the garden while her mother pruned the buddleia bush overhanging the lane. Her mother's secateurs snipped steadily. Butterflies flicked from the mauve flowers. An open car raced down the lane, accelerating as it came nearer. The driver, an airman, abruptly braked and another airman reached out of the convertible and snatched a bunch of blooms out of the buddleia, almost out of her mother's hands. The car speeded away. Her mother stood stunned. The secateurs fell from her hand. Then she burst into furious tears.

Later, remembering the act, the assault on the buddleia, Linda would allow the word 'rape' to come to mind.

---

So for Linda the idea of America in 1964 was not *appropriate*. She had entertained thoughts, lodged early by her father, an Oxford solicitor, of going to the Bar. Forced to consider George's proposition, the then Belinda Davidson of Tackley, Oxfordshire, saw herself as essentially too English for America, certainly too English for Chicago.

Chicago! She had read *The Jungle* by Upton Sinclair; she had seen the movies. She had an impression of a rotten meaty town run by meaty Irish politicians and meaty Italian criminals.

George was forced to appeal to her reason, her sense

of adventure, her idealism. He promised they would stay only three years. He pleaded. How could she deny him the chance of America? (And of marrying her, of course.) He would be at the heart of scientific research, the home of all those foundations and grants.

What was so wonderful about England, anyway? Dreary old Douglas-Home following on the heels of dreary old Macmillan. Elderly jaded Tories with their sex and spy scandals in the papers every day. The country was going to the dogs.

Then, his last card, George produced the magic letters DNA. He'd been invited to join the research program *Proteins of Agricultural, Veterinary and Technological Importance*, working in the startling new area of recombinant deoxyribonucleic acid.

'Doing what?' she asked.

'Oh, focussing initially on a vaccine for an important disease of pigs.'

She thought so. *Meat.*

'Or maybe poultry,' he said.

However, the glamor of the double helix finally wore down her resistance. It was suddenly not impossible to see George up there on the Nobel dais with Crick and Watson and Wilkins shaking the King of Sweden's hand. How could she stand in his way? They were married by the vicar of Tackley, a village known historically for its witches' covens and its proximity to Blenheim Palace, home of the Dukes of Marlborough ever since John Churchill, and within forty-eight hours they were eating pepperoni pizzas in Jackson Park while the September wind whipped froth from Lake Michigan into their faces.

To her surprise Linda took to America from the first day. She loved the vigor in the air, the contagious sense that anything was possible. While George did his research towards the production of an avian antigen vaccine (he'd

ended up with chickens after all) she studied for a graduate degree.

As she studied the American legal system she became
intrigued by its subtle and mysterious transformation
into the American political system. At home politics had
never interested her; here, ostensibly separated from class,
its ringing calls to idealism had a heady appeal. Politics
was in the hum of the freeways, in the swirling winds
off the lake. Linda became absorbed in politics.

After two years George's avian antigen research took
them on to Kansas State. By then the air currents were
crackling with politics. In Kansas in August, 1966 Linda
first spoke out against the Vietnam War at a rally called
by the Students for a Democratic Society. After an initial
nervousness she enjoyed the experience. At the rally a
self-conscious George, newly bearded, was photographed
by campus security. Next day he was warned by the dean's
office that attendance at another rally would cost him
his grant.

The threat, which dampened George's public political
ardor, further excited and radicalised Linda. It was dawn-
ing on her that she had more than her share of moral
indignation and enjoyed using it. There were meetings
and gatherings day and night. Full of ego and spirit,
she began to gather the social revolution around her
shoulders like a patchwork cloak. This patch was against
the war, that one was civil rights, this one stood for
participatory education, that one for the grape-pickers.

She would readily admit later that in those days of
strange selfless vanity she day-dreamed of being the cata-
lyst in an uprising of newly enlightened Kansans. She
saw herself as a small, fetchingly pale anti-establishment
heroine. Of this enigmatic, crisp-accented woman many
interesting rumors would be spread (the intensity of her
various campaigns was already affecting their marriage),

and on campuses around the nation love and respect for her would be tinged with awe.

The reality was both less and more romantic. She began organising for the SDS. Her increasing activism was distancing her from George. At Honey B's, an off-campus restaurant frequented by army officers, she took a part-time job as a waitress and began handing out SDS pamphlets and Quaker pacifist literature to the customers. On her third night at Honey B's George arrived to pick her up after work and was beaten up by three young lieutenants bound for Vietnam.

Next day the dean's office told the stitched and abraded George that the ban on political activity also applied to his wife. George saw his life with DNA jeopardised by her life with SDS. One set of initials was destroying the other.

'You have to make a choice,' he told her.

She agreed and left that night.

For a week she fought the longing to fly home to England, to submerge herself in cosy Oxfordshire and practise law. The feeling passed. She became a political gypsy, moving from campus to campus week by week, always just one step ahead of the Immigration Department, addressing rallies, organising, being part of things, being fed and housed and passed on with hugs and phone numbers.

In Bennington, Vermont, two months after leaving George and Kansas, she discovered she was pregnant. She wrote and told him, but gave no address. In Eugene, Oregon, she gave birth to a son, Paul. A month later, in Bolinas, northern California, she collapsed from exhaustion.

In Bolinas she was forced to rest. In 1968 the quiet coastal village was becoming a bolt-hole for the intellectually exhausted and politically wounded middle-class. Debilitated Berkeley political science professors fished for striped bass in the lagoon mouth while they caught their breath and rethought their careers. Burnt-out Haight Ashbury graduates clammed for gapers, paddled in the tidepools and thoughtfully considered the public courtship rituals of the blue heron and white egret.

Linda stayed a year in Bolinas. On a whim she sent an article and photographs on the Californian counter-culture to a London Sunday supplement. It was accepted; the payment was good. She became a freelance journalist. With her background and inclinations she chose to be an investigative reporter. Eventually it was easier to move to San Francisco rather than commute the forty miles from Bolinas. She and Paul moved in to a North Beach apartment and her life changed again.

But Linda recalled that year by the cold Pacific at Bolinas as a year of recuperation from childbirth and American fever. She let fogs and winds, geography and tides of history sweep over her. Now, with a child, she suddenly felt more connected to the past and future than to the erratic present. She showed Paul the whales spouting on their traditional migration north and sea-otters playing in the kelp. She drew pleasure from the fact that her devil-may-care compatriot Sir Francis Drake had also rested there, while adventuring around the world in the *Golden Hinde* in 1579. Remains of the fort he had built as protection against the possibility of Spanish or Indian attacks now lay at the bottom of Bolinas Lagoon.

She would sit for hours on her front porch rocking Paul's cradle and staring across the surface of the lagoon—unbroken but for the rising and settling of water-fowl—and allow herself to succumb to the gradual but revolutionary dramas of nature and landscape.

Later, when planning their escape from California, she had based her decision on her nostalgic and elemental vision of Bolinas in 1968. In her fogged despair she had agreed, even urged, that yes, they move west. The west was the traditional refuge for the wounded. Keep moving west.

# 19

In preparing profiles of the newsworthy it is believed informative to interview their old friends, their childhood playmates, if you can find them, the adolescent cronies, the people who knew them *before*.

The other pimply boy in the mailroom is generally thought to hold the secret to the rise of his old colleague to chairman of the board.

The friends of Spargo's youth were marginally more instructive than his press acquaintances. But again there was polarity of opinion.

They agreed that—and the phrase turned up more than once—he had 'a chip on both shoulders'.

They agreed that the harbour clearance at Wyndham was followed by a medal which, owing to the illegality of the explosives, his age and so forth, was somewhere between military and civilian. Apparently it was the first of many rewards, both official and sub rosa, for helpful underwater foolhardiness. After the war there were scores of other, paid, harbour clearances around the Indian Ocean and Timor Sea. There was a handy bonus from the Spanish Government for raising the galley off Ibiza.

They agreed, too, that in his life up till then he had welcomed no prize more than his introduction in the

Mediterranean in 1951 to Jacques-Yves Cousteau's revolutionary aqualung. He'd just turned twenty-one. Perhaps this was significant: he was independent and miles from home. This new scuba gear released him from the claustrophobic constraints of the bell-helmet and the dead weight of the boots. His umbilical cord was severed.

He said at the time (hoping it wouldn't be true): 'This is as good as it gets.'

At twenty-one he was as restless as he was prescient. On the off-chance that life could be even better he kept moving. In this mood of itchy anticipation he fidgeted around Europe, diving in Greece and Italy and France, working as a lifeguard in Cornwall, a swimming pool attendant in London.

His job, his swimmer's physique, the novelty of his nationality, brought many women his way. Not all of them were itinerants like himself, or even young. He was astonished to learn that his health, genial ignorance and classlessness were assets. His travels made him charming. He was reckless with his innocent élan.

It took the English winter to halt this restlessness. He thought it strangely unfair that he should pick up gonorrhea in a weekend at Brighton with a repertory actress from *Blithe Spirit*, stranger still that the disease could thrive in such cold weather. Later, England would tend to contract in his memory to extremes of temperature: from the gaseous humidity of the Chelsea Baths to Doctor Chowdhoury's draughty surgery—and icy probing fingers—in the Fulham Road.

The winter of 1952-53 had actually peaked for him one frozen afternoon in late January. He'd reeled out of the baths after work, giddy from the heat and chlorine and exercise, into the ashen cold. The air spiked his blazing cheeks. He stumbled to his boarding house in Fulham, climbed directly into bed fully dressed and fell, shivering, into deep hallucinations of Rottnest Island.

He talked often of the dream that sent him home. He was floating on his back in Little Parakeet Bay, the sun on his face and the sea in his ears. He rolled naked in powdery white sand while crows and seagulls squawked overhead. He smelled Moreton Bay figs, salt lakes and fresh bread. Endlessly he dived and swam. When he woke he smelled chlorine on the pillow, looked around and burst into tears. When he'd got over the shock of his crying he booked his passage home.

The friends of Spargo's youth could generally agree about the distant past. They agreed that he'd returned to Western Australia feeling full of experience but also more serious and self-aware. He'd looked only cursorily for a marine job on his return, and hadn't seemed disappointed when nothing suitable was available. But office jobs were plentiful. Without much effort he found himself with a position as a sales trainee at Goodyear and a serious girlfriend and the promise of a stable future.

The date that recurs in discussions of this period is Easter Sunday 1957. This date kept coming up in court as well.

In the Palace Hotel in 1964 after his first day in court Spargo said to me, 'It's laughable to think that life was ever as simple as it was then.'

We sat in the front bar watching the steam rising from St. George's Terrace. Out of the blue he mentioned Caroline Castle. It occurred to me he'd been looking for an opening. His face was flushed and mixed emotions played over it: embarrassment, pride, a touch of fear. He may have winked; maybe it was a tic.

'Off the record,' he said.

I could see why Easter Sunday 1957 loomed large in retrospect. He was really saying he couldn't believe he'd ever been twenty-seven, a family man, a keen young commercial traveller for Goodyear, totally without news interest.

He wasn't saying, not then, that if he had his life to live over again this would be the day he would take a breather and reassess the priorities.

He wasn't saying quite yet that his obsession could have ended there before it began, in a crayfisherman's boat off the south-west coast with the Doctor blowing diesoleum fumes back in his face.

That recognition came later and only subconsciously. Apart from the analysts, Rosanna was the only one who heard his dreams that it had ended there.

Eventually he no longer clearly remembered the cray-fisherman's, Clive Bullock's, face. Sometimes the features of the person on the boat were Natalie's, sometimes his mother's. Once or twice they blurred into those of old Bill Duncan, the driver's tender back in Wyndham.

'OK, that's it,' they would advise in their turn, smiling sagely. 'Call it quits.' Natalie was particularly wistful that often recreated Easter Sunday. She and the other faces spoke good sense. Hadn't he explored some new territory, speared a good fish, successfully punctuated his nine-to-five life?

He always embraced their suggestions gratefully. He kept the family together, progressed automatically at Goodyear, came to regard risk as only a hobby. His real life he simply dropped over the side of the boat.

Awake, however, he hadn't taken the hints. He'd never taken any hints, that was his trouble. All the analysts' reports said as much.

'It's still not too late,' they said, even when it was too late. 'You control it, you can fix it. Get rid of your anger,' they said. 'Feel better about your father.' His *father*?

They wanted him to moderate his principles and forget

the past. Take the olive branch. 'This is the best time in your life,' they always said, whatever age he was. In the beginning they gave him relaxation tapes to play at night, and demonstrated how to contract and relax all the main muscle groups. The toes were the place to start.

They said to put Caroline Castle right out of his mind.

# 20

This much was common knowledge. This was all in the files: it was marriage and career that brought him back to diving. It began again as a hobby. It relieved the itch of responsibility.

Revelling in its release he swam the reefs north and south of the Swan River mouth. The familiar Indian Ocean of his youth was transformed for him by the new techniques and equipment. In the sharp light before work, in the yellow summer evenings and every fine weekend he combed the underwater shoreline.

His life at this period had a fine balance to it, with a precise allotment of time. He was a husband, father, company man, a sociable man-among-men. And in his own time he was an explorer.

Rottnest, Garden, Penguin and Carnac Islands, the Stragglers, Three Mile Reef, Five Fathom Bank, he explored them all. All the time he was restlessly extending his territory and knowledge. He was always searching for the special reef, the elusive, unexplored place where the jewfish were bigger, the crayfish and abalone more plentiful, the coral more beautiful.

Competition was intensifying among the enthusiasts of this new past-time to discover these special places.

Skindivers spoke of a long reef which began ninety miles south of the river mouth and extended twenty or thirty miles further south. Somewhere along its length was a wonderful enclosed lagoon choked with fish.

Contacts on his sales route spoke of an access track to this legendary offshore lagoon. During the war the army had pushed a path through the scrub and sandhills to the coast. In the Easter holidays of 1957 he piled his diving gear into his car and set off down this sandy track.

His destination that Easter has since been vividly described and illustrated by many magazines, from *Life*, of course, to the *Women's Weekly*—its origins, its metamorphosis, even its smell of rotting crayfish.

He smelled the coast a mile before he reached it. There was a small rocky point called Thirsty Point jutting into the sea at right angles. On the sand was a collection of tin huts and five or six crayboats were moored in the bay inside the point. Around the huts lay old crayfish heads and abalone shells, and green blowflies buzzed and glistened. Broken craypots lay in the dunes. He saw, however, that to avoid cutting their bare feet the craymen had been strikingly neat with their beer bottles. A proud pyramid of them loomed behind their shacks.

He had sensibly brought along a few bottles of his own, like beads for the natives, and the beer helped him initiate a conversation with one of the craymen, a fellow named Clive Bullock. Bullock supplemented his income in the off-season by hand-lining for jewfish. The beer helped steer the talk around to skindiving.

Bullock was later quoted once as saying: 'I wouldn't put a toe in the ocean if I could help it.' He was quoted in another article as having told the reporter: 'You'd seen some of the things I'd seen, you'd never go in again. Ever see a groper's mouth up close? Ever see a white pointer take a hooked kingfish?'

The adjective 'taciturn' was applied to Bullock by one of the magazine writers. Another described him as 'typically laconic'. Bullock himself described Spargo in one interview as having 'more hide than an elephant'.

Back on Easter Sunday 1957 he had invited Spargo out in his boat and promised him schooling jewfish.

By Spargo's reckoning later, countless times later, they had motored about three miles off the coast. Then Bullock had slowed his boat over the outline of a long arm of reef. The boat was in line with a jutting limestone formation and about two miles south of Thirsty Point when they anchored.

'The sea was so still that the reef seemed only a foot below, but when I dropped the anchor, twenty, thirty, forty feet of rope followed it over the side,' Spargo said of this vital spot, this invisible X on the silver skin of the sea.

Inside the reef the lagoon reached all the way to shore. Under the boat dozens of big jewfish moved lazily. He was over-eager. Too impatient to put on his air tank or wet-suit, he quickly slipped on his fins, mask, snorkel and lead belt and slid into the water with his speargun.

He chased the fish into a tunnel in the reef. The reef here was honeycombed with tunnels and caves and weedy crevices and he thought he'd lost them. Lungs bursting, he surfaced for air and decided to swim over to where the tunnel opened out into a clear sandy space and try to catch the fish as they came out.

As he swam over the reef its appearance registered vaguely on him, the way this section shelved and shallowed abruptly under him, then suddenly altered its formation again. A tubular outcrop of coral caught his eye, then another, poking out at right angles to the reef. Just then the schooling jewfish came through the tunnel mouth and he was close enough to spear one.

Bullock's face was unimpressed when he hoisted the fish aboard. 'Hurry up. The wind's springing up.' He pointed to the waves chopping against the reef and the darkening sky in the south-west.

So the matter of the strange reef formation had waited until they were half way back to Thirsty Point.

'It wasn't a normal coral outcrop, more like the remains of a shipwreck. What do you think?' he asked Bullock.

'Dozens of ships have been wrecked along this coast. It could be any one of them. Ten, twelve fishing boats go down every year.'

Bullock is recorded in all the press articles as having then looked significantly at the weather and closed the subject.

———————

There was a wide area where the friends of Spargo's youth disagreed.

They disagreed about the detonation of certain explosions other than the one in Wyndham harbour, explosions both under water and on land.

They disagreed on the cause and effect of his fighting fifteen policemen at Shark Bay. (The fight itself was not in question.)

They disagreed on the sequence of several devastating events in the late seventies.

They even disagreed about the nature of his relationship with the Castles. But here they, like everyone else who repeated the rumours which raged from the sixties through the seventies and beyond, were only guessing.

# 21

When Spargo said it was laughable to think that life had ever been as simple as it was on Easter Sunday 1957, he was marvelling that back then Thirsty Point's most imposing edifice was a pyramid of beer bottles rising out of the dunes.

He was remembering that exploration was a fascination, not an obsession, in those days.

He was recalling a time when Perth's white collar class was welcoming him into the saloon bars of riverside hotels and to its new suburbs in the sand.

He was imagining his shipwreck as still a minute coral irregularity, a protruding speck of concretion on the limestone foundations of the continent, and his future preoccupation as still resting comfortably somewhere between myth and history.

As it was, until a week later. The week after Easter he casually mentioned the peculiar tubular protrusions off Thirsty Point to a diving and drinking companion, Dave McEntee. McEntee was a reporter for the *Daily News*. Because of his interest in skindiving he'd also made a study of the wrecks along the coast. At the mention of the strange outcrops his eyes lit up and he asked for more details.

The next day McEntee telephoned him in a state of high excitement.

'Hey, Spargo, you've discovered the *Fortuyn*!'

McEntee was in little doubt. During the war a gunner had found in the dunes some human bones, a metal plate and twenty-three Spanish coins dated between 1684 and 1718. According to historical records the *Fortuyn* had sunk somewhere nearby in 1724. Spargo's tubular coral protrusions were of course its cannons. This had to be the shipwreck.

'Listen, this is right out of *Treasure Island*,' McEntee said.

The *Fortuyn* was a Dutch merchantman which had struck a reef and sunk after being blown off course en route to Batavia. It had been carrying twelve chests of Spanish gold and silver coins to repay loans owed to the Dutch East India Company. The details were in all the shipwreck archives, McEntee assured him, even the names of the cities where the coins were minted: Mexico City, Seville and Potosi, Peru—now part of Bolivia.

Sixty per cent of the coins were eight-*real* pieces, the 'pieces of eight' beloved of Robert Louis Stevenson. The rest were silver two- and four-*real* pieces. There were three tons of coins in the chests. The cargo had to be worth millions of dollars, McEntee said.

'This is a big story,' he said.

It was the biggest local story since the Monte Bellos atom bomb tests in 1952 and the oil strike at Exmouth Gulf in 1953. (The paper had backed both these coastal news events with equal enthusiasm.)

'Don't breathe a word to anyone,' McEntee said. 'I'm going to get management support on this one.'

Within twenty-four hours Spargo was a local celebrity.

# 22

There is another school of thought which says that no-one is more instructive on the essence of newsworthiness, or at least of ambition, than the first wife (or husband).

Obviously this is journalistic territory only for those with good company lawyers. This is risky material. Certainly it can even up the ledger, but while the information can challenge, often fascinatingly, the accepted view, it tends, even in the more generous cases, to overflow into ironic comments about personal habits.

I have Natalie Spargo's account of the hours leading up to Spargo's first wave of publicity (his first *adult* tilt at celebrity) and of some preceding occurrences, their first meeting at a Goodyear Social Club barbecue and football match against Caltex in April, 1953 and so forth, but nothing at all from her later. (She refused to speak to the press after the first explosion.) This account was given at a time of relative calm before their final separation so it lacks the fine malicious edge those nerveless feature writers look for. It does, however, make an interesting contrast in tenor to her evidence at the trial.

She said it took him only five hours—from seven a.m. to noon—to become a celebrity.

At seven McEntee the reporter had arrived with a photographer on their doorstep at City Beach for the 'official' interview and photographs. Natalie made tea and toast in her dressing gown while McEntee wrote down in a notebook all the details Spargo had already told him of the unusual reef formation and the tubular coral protrusions which the reporter said were cannons.

McEntee checked his age with him and asked how he wished his occupation to be described.

'Commercial traveller.' Spargo was distracted by the boys racing round the house in their pyjamas, shrieking and showing off. 'I'm a commercial traveller.' Then he wondered aloud what Goodyear would think of all this.

'It's all good publicity,' McEntee said.

The photographer, a breezy bald man with bloodshot eyes, wanted pictures with an adventurous flavour. He asked him to put on his wet-suit in the back yard and pose for a picture hoisting an air tank on his shoulder.

Then he asked him to 'pore over an old treasure map.'

'What old treasure map?'

The photographer gave a shrewd professional grin. 'If you've got a treasure you've got to have an old treasure map.'

They settled for a Shell road map of the southern wheatbelt. Spargo got the map from the car and sat in his rubber suit at the kitchen table and was photographed studying the map.

Out of camera range Natalie prepared breakfast and John and Philip messily ate their cereal. McEntee took down their names and ages too. The toast burned. The photographer got Johnny to hold up the flash so the light would bounce off the ceiling while he snapped his father at the table. At one point the photographer stood on one of their new vinyl and chrome kitchen chairs to get a shot and Natalie's eyes widened at him but she didn't say anything.

She kept her back to the activity as much as possible. The husband she heard answering questions was unfamiliar to her. His voice was bluff and over-enthusiastic: his business voice, his sales pitch voice. She felt self-conscious in her dressing gown, dowdy and ignorant. The reporter smelled of hair oil and cigarettes and held eye contact for too long. The utensils scraped and clattered too loudly but she couldn't stop herself from making a din. Her slippers rustled on the linoleum, she never stopped hovering over her appliances but all she could come up with was tea and toast.

'Just a cuppa, thanks,' said McEntee. 'Can't face solids in the morning.'

The photographer shot a whole roll of film of Spargo at the kitchen table. Spargo covered the Shell logo with his thumb and squinted solemnly at the crosses indicating the riches of Goodyear's wheatbelt sales depots.

Then they asked him to dress quickly so they could drive him to the office of the newspaper's solicitors in the city. They said the lawyers had already drawn up salvage claims for him to sign.

'We want to look after your interests in this,' McEntee said.

When they had gone Natalie felt abruptly deflated. Drinking her tea she smelled burnt toast in her hair and cringed with embarrassment at the memory of the past two hours and the scene of bewildered domesticity they must have presented. Through clouds of smoke from burning toast she saw her dim blue figure scraping and scraping at the sink. All that feverish dressing-gowned activity at the sink! She was scraping burnt toast! She had offered the newspapermen burnt and scraped toast!

Celebrity began at midday when the first edition of the *Daily News* hit the streets. Its banner headlines announced *Fortuyn Found!* The front page was taken up by McEntee's story of the discovery and the photograph of Spargo hoisting the air tank on his shoulder barely four hours before.

The picture caption described this activity as 'preparing to recover the *Fortuyn* treasure.'

On page two there was an artist's reproduction of the state's south-west corner with a cross in the Indian Ocean just off Thirsty Point marking the *Fortuyn's* 'grave'. Beside it was a photograph of Spargo sitting at the kitchen table staring at his wheatbelt sales depots.

The caption didn't use the photographer's cliché of 'poring over an old treasure map'. Instead it said he was 'studying a chart of the shipwreck site.'

It is worth mentioning for Natalie Spargo's benefit that against the background of stippled grey newsprint the smoke from burning toast was not noticeable.

The story under McEntee's by-line mentioned all the archival material about the gold and silver *reals* the ship had been carrying. The story described the cargo as 'vast quantities of bullion' and said that Spargo, as the finder, had become an 'instant millionaire'.

It was all cut and dried. No problems were foreseen. It was just a matter of recovering the treasure.

# 23

Natalie's choice of the word 'celebrity' seems a trifle overdone. However, it should be remembered that this was a small city; she was talking of 1957. She was still in love and in awe of what she sensed was happening.

During the twenty-four hours after he became a local celebrity Spargo was talking a lot. He was frank and ebullient, drinking with reporters and making loud plans.

Then in bed that night, with the sweet acetone smell of alcohol coming through his skin, he was tender and sentimental.

'I'm in two minds about all this,' he confessed to her.

He enjoyed basking in the limelight, no doubt about it. It was a heady sensation. He felt invulnerable and his horizons seemed endless. But he was being swept along by the momentum of 'news'. It was 'news' that had granted him sudden importance and there was little he could do about it.

So he felt alternately powerful and impotent, famous and less than nobody.

But the next day he had blithely dropped all his work and domestic responsibilities to satisfy the requirements of the media. Their requirements were brutally simple:

they wanted the treasure recovered, they wanted it recovered *now* and they wanted it recovered in front of their eyes exclusively.

It was a lesson for Natalie. 'From that moment on we were pushed into the background,' she said.

But put yourself in Spargo's place, carried along by the tide of your own quoted remarks and photographed actions. There are your malleable words, rearranged and set down for posterity. There is your likeness, allegedly brave and imaginative, 'preparing to recover the *Fortuyn* treasure' and 'studying a chart of the shipwreck site'.

It was impossible not to surge forward, much less pause to think or sensibly postpone the momentum for any reason—until the weather was more suitable, for example. (Since the evening before the coast had been battered by wind and rain.)

He knew that diving conditions would be bad at present; this was obvious from the strong westerlies and rain squalls. But when he pointed this out, McEntee shrugged.

'They really want this one,' he said.

And, now, so did he. He couldn't argue. The day after the story broke he found himself driving rapidly south to Thirsty Point with McEntee and two other newsmen, one an underwater photographer and the other a younger reporter and experienced skindiver, in a Land-Rover supplied and equipped by the newspaper. They towed a trailer carrying a fifteen-foot dinghy and a fifty-horsepower outboard engine.

Rain dashed against the windscreen as they left the highway and bumped down the old army track to the coast. High swells generated far out to sea were sweeping towards land and exploding against the point.

At some time during the journey it must have become clear to Spargo that he was caught in a cross-current.

Some things would also become clear to the newsmen on that assignment. There were lessons for everyone on that job. For example, everyone remembered the faking of the cannon. It was the faking of the cannon that reporters would bring up in pubs years later, that and the hollow ghostly whistling of the wind through the bottle heap.

Reporters have their legends and superstitions too. To hear some of them talk it was as if the faking of the cannon brought on its own retribution.

At Thirsty Point the six or seven crayfishermen in residence came out of their shacks and watched as the press team unloaded the Land-Rover and pitched tents in the lee of the bottle heap. The craymen watched them lash flapping tarpaulins over their cartons of food, their bedding, tables and camp chairs, their cooking and eating utensils, the icebox, stove and gas supply. The craymen stood steaming quietly in the rain, cigarettes sheltered in cupped hands, taking in the air compressor and hoses, the aqualung equipment, the rubber suits and lead belts and fins and spearguns and face masks, the bags of underwater photographic apparatus, the dinghy and outboard.

'Going diving, boys?' inquired Clive Bullock. 'I wouldn't recommend it.'

However, there was to be no diving for some time. The press party sat morosely on the beach and waited out the weather. They played poker and pontoon with the craymen and woke every morning with hangovers to the whistling of the westerly in the bottle heap. Each morning at seven McEntee held a fractured conversation with his editor on the Land-Rover's two-way radio, consisting mainly of *Roger* and *Over* and *Do you receive me?* (The editor loved using the two-way radio but always inadvertently cut himself off the air.) But after a week with no story other than variations on *Weather Beats Treasure Hunter*, his patience was running out.

The party's patience, too, was stretched to breaking point. For eleven days the sea was too rough for them to venture beyond the bay. They huddled in their tents against the gritty wind, their tempers edgy, McEntee taking the weather personally and Spargo retreating within himself. They were in a frustrating bind: they weren't able to dive on the wreck and yet they couldn't return to town. Having trumpeted the *Fortuyn's* discovery, they were forced to squat in the sand at Thirsty Point to guard the wreck from possible intruders.

Then, on the twelfth morning, they woke to sunshine and an extraordinary silence. The wind had dropped, the whistling had ceased. On the two-way radio McEntee briefed the editor: 'We're diving today.' He dictated a story for that afternoon's edition: fortune was finally smiling on the patient *Fortuyn* team. At last they were diving on the wreck. Valuable discoveries awaited them. He talked again in millions. Pieces of eight. The next few days would prove just how rich was Spargo's find.

To the party this wasn't even hyperbole. Spargo, McEntee, everyone, was suddenly charged with optimism. They had always taken it for granted that Bullock would simply lead them back to the wreck site and they would begin diving. But as they loaded their gear aboard his boat and readied to leave, Bullock remarked laconically, 'Well, I hope I can find the spot again.'

McEntee threw Spargo an appalled glance. During the trip south over the reef they hardly dared speak.

They motored three miles off the coast and two miles south of Thirsty Point. Spargo looked for the jutting limestone headland and Bullock moved the boat into line with it.

They anchored. In the absence of wind there were no waves and the boat sat silent and motionless on the surface. Spargo marvelled suddenly at the imprecision of his alignments. The sheer amplitude and impartiality of the sea filled him with awe. He could only put on his scuba gear and slip over the side, away from the blank faces.

He dived over coral outcrops, sloping reefs and limestone caverns, swam back and forth all morning. He recognised none of them. This wasn't the place.

He couldn't find the *Fortuyn*.

McEntee put it simply. 'I can't face the editor without a shipwreck.' Spargo had to keep the story alive while they continued to search. The photographer decided to take a photograph of Spargo sawing through a cannon-shaped limestone solution pipe, a natural marine phenomenon in the area. The caption on the published picture said: 'Treasure-hunter Don Spargo frees what he believes is an 18th century Dutch cannon.'

What *he* believes. Transferring the onus for the lie on to him.

They continued to search and found nothing. Then the weather broke and the ocean swells rose again and smashed against the point. They had no choice but to break camp and return to the city.

On the return trip McEntee spoke only once to Spargo. 'What do you think this makes me look like?' he said.

---

The newspaper made no explanation to its readers for its abrupt change of heart on the *Fortuyn* story. It dropped the story like a hot coal and allowed it to fizzle out. One or two readers wondered in letters to the editor whether Spargo was being cagey. They surmised that he had had second thoughts and shrewdly wanted to keep his discovery secret. Several others, reflecting the majority, took the paper's sudden rejection of him to mean he was either a liar or a boastful fool. The paper didn't disabuse them.

Natalie bore his humiliation with him for six months and would, I believe, have continued to bear with him.

But his humiliation was deep and all-encompassing. It was increased by the same factor that had enhanced his brief celebrity—the smallness and insularity of the community.

'Where's the treasure, Don?'

He knew everyone and felt they were all laughing or sneering. On the street their smiles were too broad for him to bear. He crossed the road to avoid a wink from a familiar face. His skin was too thin for the banter of the pubs. The office, his country sales route, were a nightmare of embarrassment and tension.

'Where's the treasure, Don?'

He bore it for six months. When the crayfish season opened he resigned from Goodyear and drove down to Thirsty Point and asked Bullock if he needed an offsider.

He lived in a one-roomed tin shed behind the bottle heap. He rose at three every morning in all weathers and waded out to Bullock's boat with sacks of rotting fish for crayfish bait. Then they hefted drums of diesoline aboard. At three-thirty they headed out in the pitching swells over the reefs where he pulled craypots, emptied, baited and set craypots until noon.

Every morning he was sea-sick. Every fine afternoon he searched for the *Fortuyn*.

His marriage, of course, was also foundering on the reefs off Thirsty Point.

# 24

For all its staying power as a conversation topic, what is meant by 'the Spargo affair' in Perth today depends very much on whom you talk to.

The press, once it had got over the sentiment angle, the luck angle, the adventure angle, of this outdoor boy eventually finding the *Fortuyn* again five years later, soon swung its attention from the heroics to the legal and financial aspects (which were certainly complex enough), became bored with them and settled on the clashes with authority.

However, to the social network, especially to that group of female lunchers and tennis players which still remembered with cheery phone calls the birthdays of their private-school partners from the Friday night classes at the Linley Wilson School of Ballroom Dancing in 1953, the big story, the only story, was the one set in train on the Castles' terrace overlooking the river in December 1962.

There were of course witnesses other than Leon Levinson that night; people who, in retrospect, were also able to draw a continuous line from cause to effect.

But there had been no witnesses after two in the morning. Spargo and Levinson had been the last to leave the party—at one thirty. Castle was busy on the phone to London and Tokyo and Caroline had insisted on driving the two guests home. The three of them had piled into the car's front seat.

'Very chummy.'

As Spargo recalled in the front bar of the Palace Hotel in 1964 while outside the street steamed in the rain. He still shook his head at the memory. Perhaps he still couldn't believe it. Perhaps he was still unsettled by his first day in court. He remembered that as she backed the Mercedes up the drive to the road there was a single pin-point of yellow light, possibly a prawner's lamp, down on the black river.

He remembered it was two o'clock when they dropped the jet-lagged Levinson at the Esplanade Hotel and watched his wobbly progress into the foyer.

He remembered the instantly changed, deeply intimate atmosphere in the car.

He remembered her smiling silence behind the wheel, her uptilted profile and its slow half-turn towards him when they reached his flat on the ocean front at Cottesloe. He, too, half-turned towards her, to thank her. Obviously they had been drinking, but time was now drawn out. It seemed to him that things were in a delicate balance. Life was finely tuned and every millisecond counted for something. He was turning to thank her but he was actually hesitating from opening the door. In this fraction of a moment he heard the waves breaking on the shore and the breeze from the sea fizzing through the Norfolk pines.

'Goodnight,' he said.

But his hand was still not quite connecting with the door handle. At the same time she was not positioned entirely correctly for driving away. Her hands were not on the wheel. Her position was just a shade less than ambiguous. She was sitting with her back against the driver's door, looking steadily at him.

Even as he moved the vast distance across the seat to her, he was thinking, 'What's got into me?' As he kissed her it struck him (and his cheeks still glowed to tell me) that he was making a dreadful mistake: all the momentum, all the kiss's energy was coming from him. Her mouth was cool and passive. Of course this didn't discourage him. Of course the recklessness she had already signalled that night was soon evident. Her initial quiescent reaction was only, literally, paying lip service to the conventions of her class and era. Private-school boys. The Linley Wilson School of Ballroom Dancing. Growing up in the fifties.

I gathered that this was part of the fascination.

'These girls have their little rules,' Spargo told me.

———————

Once Spargo had well and truly found his treasure, the general view of him as a vexatious litigant, as a troublesome thorn in society's side, tended to take over.

Within six months people began using phrases like 'dog in the manger' in relation to his possessive attitude to the wreck. And people began talking of explosives again. It was recalled that he had precociously bombed the freighter in Wyndham harbour with a hundred pounds of *plastique*. Illegal explosives. In wartime.

The papers implied that his fondness for gelignite as a salvage tool was blowing the *Fortuyn* to smithereens. They talked as if the *Fortuyn* was a perfectly preserved ship and he was bombing it to rubble. In the Palace Hotel the reporters laughed that he didn't always wait for everyone to get out of the water.

Spargo threatened the papers with libel suits. He

obtained an injunction of restraint and the gelignite stories stopped for a while.

'I calculate exactly what is required,' he complained to me on the way from the Supreme Court to the Palace Hotel in 1964.

But Spargo was definitely not, in the jargon of marine salvage circles, 'a quarter-stick man.' He was not even 'a full-stick man.' He was 'a six-stick man.'

And the stories had their effect. The state passed the Maritime Archeology Act specifically to take the *Fortuyn* from him. The law protected all the shipwrecks along the coastline and handed over their contents to the State Museum. The law was made retrospective; it forbade him from exploring or even entering the area of the wreck, or salvaging materials from it without permission. He had to pass over to the museum any artifacts or articles which it wanted from the material he had already salvaged.

He reacted characteristically. He challenged the law, unsuccessfully, in the Supreme Court. 'Who do they think they're dealing with?' he said as we strode along St. George's Terrace. The deep humiliated flush was on his face. 'I've stood under water shovelling bullion into bags until the sweat ran through my wet-suit,' he said.

I took him to mean that he had the stamina to carry the fight through the courts. I thought he was also boasting that he had already shovelled five or six thousand pieces of eight into a vault at the Bank of New South Wales and that anyone would be lucky to prise a single coin from him.

I had no inkling of the extent of his obstinacy. Neither did I guess that this first day in court had seen the last agreement, the only accord, he would have with authority again.

## 25

On his first day in court Spargo and the State agreed on the historical facts of the *Fortuyn* shipwreck. The facts presented to the court were as follows:

The *Fortuyn* had struck a reef off the coast of the Southland, of what would become Western Australia, on 2 May, 1724. The ship belonged to the *Vereenigde Oost-Indische Compagnie*, the Dutch East India Company. The State of the Netherlands, by virtue of the 1798 Constitution of the Batavian Republic, was the present legal successor to the Company.

Batavia, now Jakarta, on the island of Java, was the centre of this immense trading company, whose operations extended from Persia to Japan. To maintain its operations in the East the Company required a regular supply of ships, men, money and goods from the Netherlands.

It had spent fifty years in defining the quickest, safest and cheapest route to the Indies. Following investigations by the explorer Hendrik Brouwer, the Company ordered all its ships bound for the Indies to sail the quicker southern route from the Cape of Good Hope. This involved sailing south from the Cape to approximately latitude 36 degrees, then following the Roaring

Forties east towards the Southland until the master estimated he was due south of the Sunda Strait, when he
would head north for Batavia.

On 27 September, 1723, the *Fortuyn* had sailed from
Texel on her maiden voyage to Batavia. Her master was
Pieter Westrik and she had a crew of two hundred and
twenty-five men. The ship was a medium-sized merchantman, weighing two hundred and eighty tons and one
hundred and forty-five feet long. It was recorded that
she carried three tons of the Company's treasure, amount-
ing to three hundred and twenty thousand guilders and
trade goods valued at one hundred thousand guilders.

After a week at the Cape of Good Hope the *Fortuyn*
sailed on 18 January, 1724, following Brouwer's route
south and east. On 2 May, at the start of the first day-
watch, in full sail with a following wind, she struck
the reef off the Southland so violently that 'she was
immediately burst open and sunk down' with only her
stern projecting above water. Most of the crew, at least
one hundred and forty men, were trapped below in their
sleeping quarters and drowned.

Seventy-five survivors, including Master Westrik, his
understeersman and six women passengers, reached the
shore. All that was saved from the ship was one sound
boat and a few provisions and kegs of water.

Master Westrik ordered the understeersman to take six
sailors and sail the boat to Batavia for help. Two sailors
died of thirst but the understeersman reached Batavia
safely six weeks later. The Company immediately sent
a quick-sailing flyboat, the *Goede Hoop*, to the Southland to try to recover the survivors and the treasure.

The weather on the south-west coast was stormy, with
strong north-easterly winds and a high surf along the
shoreline, but the *Goede Hoop* managed to land one
of its boats. Once on shore, however, three members of

the search party wandered into the bush and disappeared. Eight men sent in search of them were drowned when their boat was dashed to pieces on the reef. Altogether, thirteen of the *Goede Hoop's* crew died searching for the *Fortuyn's* survivors, including two fifteen-year-old boys who were marooned and left to die on two separate rocky islands as a punishment for homosexuality.

Storms and high seas prevented the ship from continuing its search and she returned to Batavia having found no trace of the *Fortuyn* or its survivors.

In Batavia the Company decided that any further search should wait for the calmer weather of summer. Six months later a second rescue expedition was mounted in the galliot *Weseltje*. The forty-man vessel was provisioned for six months. Firm sailing instructions and a strict code of moral behaviour were issued, as well as orders to chart the coast of the Southland and investigate possible trading contacts with the 'Indians'. As an incentive it was announced that a proportion of any treasure recovered from the wreck would be shared among the crew.

The *Weseltje* sighted the Southland on 24 February, 1725 at about latitude 34 degrees. From this point she sailed north along the coast carrying out soundings and constructing a chart. On 8 March at about 33° 52′ the crew sighted a fire ashore which, on the firing of signal guns, was answered by another fire. A boat was sent ashore and the search party was met by a small band of 'Indians'. The Aborigines were amiable but their 'primitive' habitation, lack of possessions and apparent lack of understanding of their mission disappointed the Dutchmen. No trace of the *Fortuyn's* survivors or wreckage was discovered.

On 20 March at 33° 20′ the master sent his uppersteersman and fourteen men ashore where they found a wooden beam believed to have come from the *Fortuyn*. Their boat was sent back again next day. During the afternoon a south-west gale blew up and when the boat had not returned the following day it was assumed to have sunk. The *Weseltje* managed with difficulty to beat off the lee shore and make for the open sea.

Next afternoon a fire was seen on shore, and on the *Weseltje's* firing a signal gun, another fire was lit. This was assumed to be 'the work of Christians', either of the ship's boat or from the *Fortuyn*. The ship hove to during the night but there was no suitable anchorage and without a boat no men could be landed. In the morning the ship was found to have drifted north and, concerned that it would founder on the reefs, the master decided to sail back to Batavia.

Meanwhile, the uppersteersman and the boat's crew, who had indeed lighted the signal fires, waited helplessly on the beach for eleven days hoping that the ship would return. When it did not the crew patched up the boat, which had lost its rudder on the reefs, and on 8 April, with provisions of seal meat, seaweed and ten gallons of rain water collected during the storm, set sail for Batavia.

On the long journey three crew died of thirst and for two weeks before reaching land the others were forced to drink sea water. On reaching the Java coast the upper-steersman sent five men who could swim ashore to collect food and water, but having satisfied their own thirst and hunger they refused to rejoin the boat. The remaining two men who could swim were sent ashore and acted in a similar manner.

The uppersteersman was forced to sail on. The next day, because of the exhausted state of the remaining crew, the boat was wrecked in the surf. After struggling through the jungle these four men eventually arrived in Batavia, barely alive, five months later.

In the light of the two disastrous rescue missions, the Governor-General of Batavia and the Company decided to have done with further attempts to recover either the survivors or the treasure of the *Fortuyn*.

For a century the documents relating to the *Fortuyn* remained in the State Archives in Holland while the British established the Swan River Colony on the coast of Western Australia one hundred miles north of the area where the ship had foundered.

In 1944 Gunner William Hurst found twenty-three silver coins in the sand hills at Thirsty Point. Their dates, ranging between 1684 and 1718, indicated that they could have come from survivors of the *Fortuyn*.

In 1957 a diver, the plaintiff Donald Patrick Spargo, reported that he had discovered the wreck of the *Fortuyn* off Thirsty Point. However, a further search of the vicinity failed to find any trace of the wreck.

On 26 November, 1962 Donald Spargo discovered the wreck lying on an off-shore reef 2.8 miles from the coast of Western Australia at latitude 33° 30′ south, longitude 115° 50′ east and at all times submerged in the sea.

The reef is limestone with numerous solution holes, caves, tunnels and channels. Except on the sand-shingle floors of these caves it is extremely difficult to distinguish the wreck material from the bedrock. The only wreck materials noticeable on the site are the heavily concreted and weeded cannon and anchors. Most of the wreck is covered with sea-grass and algae. Numbers of small yellow bricks are scattered over the area, and closer examination reveals some pottery, brass candlesticks, coins and ivory.

Excavation on the wreck site is difficult. The material

is welded to the reef and the wreck is exposed to the Indian Ocean swell. The weather conditions are unpredictable and any high swell makes working on the wreck very hazardous.

———————

There was another historical fact, a fact later revealed to another court whose sitting was not made public.

After the party he had pressed an eight-*real* coin into her hand, a piece of eight minted in Seville in 1685.

She wore it on a chain around her neck until, as near as could be estimated, 4.07 p.m. on 12 September, 1979.

# 26

An interesting thing about Spargo's and Rosanna's type of relationship—the older (distracted) man and the ingénue—was that he could leave her pregnant and stranded like a beached whale and yet treat her as his greatest confidante.

For example, Rosanna knew all about Caroline Castle, or at least as much as he felt able to confide.

She knew and tried to understand his pig-headedness, his impulses for high public recognition and for retaliatory adventures.

More than anyone Rosanna was privy to his fears. Only to her would he confess his fear of death—and mention the method of dying he most dreaded. At first she thought he was joking. It was such a silly, accidental, almost laughable form of death. It wasn't one or other of the unholy coronary-stroke-cancer trinity, nor an underwater hazard like sharks or equipment failure. What agitated Spargo, she told me, was the idea of random death by jellyfish.

Two or three years before he had read of a small jellyfish slipping down the throat of a famous swimmer, and the image, the imagined sensation, had affected him strongly. He recalled the countless times he'd swum through swarms of jellyfish and not given them a thought. It wasn't even a particularly venomous jellyfish that had killed the swimmer, but its tentacles had stung the inside of his throat and, what with him panicking and inhaling water and the rapidly swelling lesions choking him, he had died within minutes.

Only Rosanna knew that since reading about the swimmer swallowing the jellyfish—and it had happened some place far off, Colombo or Durban or somewhere—Spargo hadn't swum again, at least not for pleasure. He'd only enter the water protected by his wet-suit and with the mouthpiece of his air-supply clenched in his teeth.

While Rosanna was privy to his fears, she wasn't privy to his distant past. She had no way of knowing that this sort of eccentric anxiety—the worry of death by jellyfish ingestion, not to mention the bail jumping, the shadowy acquaintances, the illegal schemes—would once have been completely foreign to his nature. She didn't know that something vital was missing. She presumed that the raw and vulnerable edge to his character had always been there, that she was seeing the complete man, not only the man who had always been, but the man at his peak.

And if this was it, the complete Spargo, she reasoned, not only was she in competition with the other women of his life, the women of his past—Caroline and Natalie— but she had beaten them. He was, after all, with her (most of the time). She was carrying his child. He was a famous and unusual man and he had chosen her. It hadn't taken her long to forgive him for disappearing.

'His emotional system was overloaded. It was inevitable some little wire would disconnect,' she told me.

She couldn't afford to consider the alternative. And if he had momentarily blown a fuse he had at least been in control of events again, leading the merry dance instead of being led, so that by the time they were back in court she found him quieter in spirit, subdued and affectionate during the lunch adjournments and her weekend visits to him in Long Bay.

Her bail hadn't been affected of course. Even the most suspicious detectives on the case had been convinced by her pregnancy and panic that she knew nothing about his disappearance. During the committal hearing she was still staying with the Marriotts at Drummoyne, awaiting the baby and attending the Sydney Court of Petty Sessions each day while the police outlined to the magistrate their reasons for bringing the charges and Spargo and a procession of solicitors attempted to rebut the police evidence.

Rosanna's account separates here, like whey and curds, into fact and non-fact. There was her court evidence, in the compulsory form of such evidence: her answers to strictly specific questions put to her by each side and taken down by the court typist (and reported in greatly abbreviated form, with a different emphasis, in the next morning's papers). That was the fact, the thin milky whey of events.

There was also her subjective account, to me, to others, to anyone who would listen to her after 16 February, 1984. This was the area of non-fact, the inadmissable evidence, the surreal hearsay. The creamy curds.

It doesn't follow that if something is non-fact it is necessarily false, only that it has no validity in legal or journalistic circles. In life, of course, even in the 'real world' so constantly conjured up by pragmatic lawyer-politicians and editorial writers, the area of non-fact controls and conditions the majority of decisions and responses.

There was the non-fact of the dream Spargo described

to Rosanna one lunch break towards the end of the committal proceedings while they ate a sandwich and drank takeaway coffee.

After his absconding on bail, the desert adventure-turned-sour, the capture, when he wasn't yet used to being locked up every night, he'd had this recurrent nightmare.

The cell was a diving bell. Deceptively, for a second, this was a relief. So that's why he was here! Of course, just a professional visit. An oil rig. His job was to check the spudding-in of the drill. Pressure gauges, depth meters and silver pipes sprouted from the walls. The walls were steel. The floor was steel. His mind's eye focussed on all that steel. There was a porthole on each of the four walls, opaque and murky, with only a milky green light coming through. The bell's door clanged shut on him and the steel resounded as the bell lurched, rocked and then swung out over the sea.

He began to descend. He was alone, although un-named, faceless men operated the winch and air supply above him. He opened the air cocks and watched the needles on the depth gauge rise. Fifty, seventy, one hundred feet. He was waiting for it. Then he saw the small inevitable trickle of water coming from a floor weld. One hundred and fifty. Two hundred. The water now began to spurt in, spraying against the opposite wall. Gushing.

Emerging from these dreams was difficult, especially when the light from the corridor outside revealed surroundings barely less desperate, and his waking consciousness registered simultaneously the fact, the smell, the word. *Jail.*

Once more there was the steel bunk under him, the stainless steel sink, the seatless lavatory in the corner, his portable Olivetti on a small table, the stacks of books and papers for his defence.

Nothing else. Even his clothes for court: the grey Anthony Squires suit, three white shirts and choice of ties (a sombre maroon and a navy blue), the black brogues he'd bought at Ezywalkin for Rosanna's sister Beverley's wedding, were kept in the locker room near the showers. He had no sentimental photographs or bright prints or mementoes or pin-ups, nothing personal or decorative.

Why not soften the crude edges of jail as Rosanna had suggested? No, this would suggest, to himself as well as others, that somehow he accepted the situation. He said he pitied the old lifers and weak-minded tattooed youths with their walls of nude centrefolds, their frilly curtains, fish tanks and carpet squares, their proud book-cases made of fruit boxes to hold their Phantom comics and Penthouses and car magazines. It was important to fight the idea of permanence; to do otherwise would water down his defence, perhaps even hint at an admission of guilt.

'They watch for things like that,' he insisted.

Waking cold with sweat he'd try to stage his re-adjustment calmly and slowly. Slow breaths to calm the heart. Avoid panic and rise gradually to the surface. Decrease the pressure. Recompression was vital.

When the water in the diving bell rose to his chest, then his neck, he was forced to fight for his life. And this was where he blossomed, he told Rosanna proudly. He shrewdly fought back with beauty.

He would switch off the nightmare by switching on the diving bell's floodlights. He survived by creating sudden beauty out of the murk. In his light the plankton became billions of boisterous sparks, and from the vision of their dazzling play, their wild and teeming incandescence, he drew some sort of optimism.

It is tempting to pass Rosanna's reported non-fact through one's own filter of intuitive imagination, one's own reading of the facts. Perhaps there was something erotic about this brilliant explosion. And something else that went so close to the impulses of his brain, his electricity, his essence of self, that he could smell the final acrid powder.

The 'something else'. He would have been familiar with the 'something else', the sensation he experienced during the brain examinations, the scans, the EEGs, the X-rays, the electrodes on his scalp; the catheter pushed into the groin and the tube fed up, up, high into the head, the hot fluid into the corners of the brain, four times, the boiling flush in his head, the fruitless search for abnormalities. And behind his eyes his brain reacted and recreated the explosion of the luminous sizzling plankton.

And then there was the sweet tranquil fear. Unsettling rather than terrifying. An awareness that ecstasy and oblivion were connected by just a... thread. Just the feathery brush of two wires.

———————

With her his pleasure was so intense that these wild glowing pinpoints not only filled his head but exploded out through his eyes and projected themselves on to external surfaces. They danced on the bedroom wall, the bedstead, the ceiling, the pillow, and flickered on the pale receptive screen of the soft body arched against him.

They lay without words, shining wet, on top of the covers in the guest bedroom overlooking the terrace where it had started. Four o'clock insanity. A couple of small seascapes looked down on their recklessness; photographed VIPs smiled a blind eye. The river was in the edge of the window, a speck of feathery cloud, a white gum branch.

His moisture shone on her while she herself (younger, crisper-coiffed, evening-gowned; in the company of her tuxedoed husband and several grinning Japanese men) smiled down on them. There a deal consummated. Here, well, the piece of eight—smoothed and lightened by two centuries under the sea—lay between her glistening breasts and he balanced it on his finger.

# 27

While Caroline Castle was asleep for ten days between 11 March and 21 March, 1979, Spargo won a rare victory not twenty miles from her.

Narcotised as she was in the leafy outer reaches of Sydney's North Shore, she had no way of knowing that on 15 March he had, by the slenderest of margins, finally succeeded in reversing the law which had taken the *Fortuyn* from him fifteen years before.

The High Court, sitting in Sydney, with the Chief Justice using his casting vote in a split three-three decision, declared that the State Act which had seized the wreck and its contents in 1964 was invalid.

Comatose on the North Shore (though her brain was electrically convulsed, under her psychiatrist's—the Martian's—instructions, by Sister Yvonne Chung on the mornings of 13, 15 and 17 March), Caroline Castle could not have read the thoughtful feature article by the legal correspondent of the *Sydney Morning Herald* which discussed how Spargo's victory had thrown into question the offshore laws of the world's largest island.

The writer said the 'historic decision' meant that the seabed and everything on it were no longer subject to the legislative power of a State. The decision was a very important legal interpretation of relative State and Commonwealth rights and would have many repercussions, particularly for offshore oil drilling.

Spargo had highlighted for the oil companies and governments the administrative vacuum over the nation's seaboard.

The article summed up the 'complex legal argument' which had echoed through the courts for the past fifteen years, indeed since the June day in Perth in 1964 when Spargo and I walked from the Supreme Court to the Palace Hotel in the light rain; when steam rose from St. George's Terrace and he told me off the record that Caroline Castle always had tears in her eyes.

I thought the phrase 'complex legal argument' was severely understating the case. For example, 'complex legal argument' didn't encompass the matter of the small ballast brick of yellow clay which Spargo blithely gave Leon Levinson as a souvenir when he showed him over the *Fortuyn* wreck in 1962, and which was in Levinson's hands—the usual photographer's prop—in the photograph illustrating my interview with him in *The West Australian.*

Nor did the phrase cover the fight with the fifteen policemen at Shark Bay when they 'apprehended' Spargo over the ballast brick incident.

And in no way did 'complex legal argument' cover the eight-*real* coin, minted in Seville in 1685, which Caroline Castle wore between her breasts for more than sixteen years.

Consider 'complex legal argument' as a euphemism for trouble, for a bureaucratic rough-and-tumble of which only chronology can attempt to make sense.

Once the State law had been passed in 1964 to take the *Fortuyn* from Spargo, events had quickly gathered momentum. This was the period which he would later refer to as the time of his and my 'working relationship'; in fact, a time of tense late night phone calls and excitable 'scoops' as he liked to call his defamatory midnight news suggestions.

The day after the bill was passed he called on the museum director in her dark jarrah-panelled office above the main display floor of stuffed bison and moulting llamas and dioramas of Aboriginal hunting and campfire scenes. The museum director, a portly Englishwoman with a doctorate in anthropology, regarded him uncomfortably, self-conscious in her victory: the *Fortuyn* had been placed in her hands but she seemed unsure what to do with her prize.

'Well,' Spargo said, 'I've already recovered a ton-and-a-half of Spanish coins in conglomerate, an anchor, an astrolabe, four cannons, six bronze statues, ivory and 5,600 ballast bricks. What do you want me to do with them?'

The museum director's first instinct was for peace and quiet. 'Mr. Spargo,' she said soothingly, 'I know we are of one mind on this.'

'Also fifteen bellarmine jugs,' he went on, 'twelve brass candlesticks, fifty cannonballs, a mortar and pestle and a pair of sailmaker's scissors.'

The museum director was at pains to stress that she didn't want him to be disadvantaged. 'We're just instructed to protect the *Fortuyn* for posterity,' she said. 'We can't possibly use all this stuff.' Of the material he'd already salvaged the museum required only a selection from each category. That included the coins. 'We'll need a small sample for display. The rest are yours. You'll be a rich man.' Moreover, she would like to hire him and his boat and diving equipment to help salvage the rest of the cargo.

Spargo was partly mollified. He agreed to take the

museum salvage party to Thirsty Point a week later. The party, led by a marine archaeologist named Gerard Grant, and also comprising two divers and a carpenter, upheld the traditions of the crayfishing settlement by arriving with a big supply of beer, wine and spirits. Six nights passed in heavy drinking and bawdy songs; six mornings of fine diving weather were wasted in headachy remorse.

Spargo kept his distance from this naughty boys' picnic. He kept himself fit with daily swimming and jogging, he readied his equipment and waited for Grant to start the official salvage work. But after a week the only instructions Grant had given were for the carpenter to build a raft. His plan was to float the raft over the *Fortuyn* and haul the artifacts and coins aboard with a block and tackle.

Spargo argued with him. 'The reason we're here is because the Indian Ocean sinks ships. What do you think our chances are of anchoring a lumbering bloody raft out there?'

Grant disagreed. The next day the raft was completed and launched, amid much boozy jollity, with a bottle of beer against its side. Overnight it was anchored offshore. The usual evening easterly was blowing over the point and out to sea. Next morning the raft had vanished.

'What do we do now?' Grant wondered.

'Why not put a *Lost* ad in a South African newspaper,' said Spargo. His patience was running out. 'We'll go out in my boat and do it my way.' It was only when he and the two museum divers were treading water over the wreck and waiting for Grant, the underwater expert, to join them and direct the operation that they discovered he couldn't swim.

Spargo climbed back into his boat, summoned the other divers aboard, motored back to Thirsty Point, packed up his gear and drove back to town. Flushed and waving his arms about, he was in the newsroom of *The West Australian* dictating this episode to me the same evening.

Even the circumspect version which appeared in the paper next morning ruffled a few feathers. Spargo didn't mind. Through me he was going public. He had discovered his voice and seemed to enjoy using it. He progressed rapidly to the more vehement and personal media—radio and television—and used them to underline his point. The State had legal control of the *Fortuyn* but it couldn't physically control it. Every fine day looters and pilferers were diving on the wreck under the nose of the protector. Meanwhile, Grant and his team had been sent abroad to study treasure salvaging techniques in the Mediterranean and Caribbean. At the taxpayers' expense.

Spargo was a media favourite again. 'Maybe Mr. Grant can get some swimming lessons in the Caribbean,' he deadpanned for them. The public scoffed with him.

———————

I recall a question I had for him during this period. 'The raft?' I wondered.

'Off the record?' he asked.

'I suppose so,' I sighed.

'What do you think? It was a windy night,' he laughed. 'I hope you don't think I untied any knots.'

# 28

One day in late 1964 Spargo arrived at the museum with a truckload of ballast bricks from the *Fortuyn*. 'Here you are,' he told the director. 'I hope you've got room for them.'

The director said, very evenly, 'We have more than enough, thank you,' and had the load dumped at the city garbage tip.

Before he left the museum premises Spargo decided to check on the material he had already handed over. In the basement where the articles were being sorted and cleaned for exhibition he discovered that five of the bellarmine jugs had been accidentally smashed. His astonished reaction made the broken jugs another pithy little news item.

However, it was the *Fortuyn's* ballast bricks, and one small yellow clay brick in particular, which made news in the coming months.

*Ballast* is defined as a heavy substance used to improve the stability and control the draft of a ship. Similarly, it is something that gives stability to character or conduct, a sense of responsibility.

The definition seemed particularly ironic at key points over the next fifteen years.

At 6.30 a.m. on the day after my small story on the broken bellarmine jugs appeared in the *The West Australian*, Detective-Sergeant Russell Sikes stood at the doorway of Spargo's flat thumping the door with his fist.

When Spargo sleepily opened the door, Sergeant Sikes pushed a photostated copy of a newspaper page in his face. It was my interview with Levinson on his visit for NASA and *Life* almost two years before. The page also showed the photograph of him holding the ballast brick.

The sergeant prodded the photograph with a finger. 'Did you give this man that brick he's holding?'

'Yes, why?'

'In that case I'm arresting you for a breach of the Maritime Archeology Act. You will accompany me to headquarters and be duly charged.'

'Like hell I will! That was two years ago. Anyway, I've just given the museum five thousand bricks and they dumped them on the garbage tip.'

'If you refuse to come with me, we'll take you forcibly,' the sergeant said, nodding towards the car from which another three policemen were emerging.

'Let me get dressed then.'

Sergeant Sikes gripped the sleeve of Spargo's pyjama coat. 'You'll come now.'

At the police station he was charged with having illegally disposed of a relic, to wit a ballast brick of historic interest from the vessel *Fortuyn*, in breach of the Maritime Archeology Act. The unusual nature of the charge meant a long and embarrassing delay in the charge room while police clerks languidly checked the relevant act in statute books, poured themselves cups of tea, sought further opinions from colleagues and wandered in and out of the room with their arms full of books and charge sheets.

Stirring sugar into his tea, Sergeant Sikes laconically oversaw this slow to-ing and fro-ing. Each time another policeman came into the room the new man would look Spargo up and down and mutter some witticism about his pyjamas, and Sikes would say, with a chuckle, 'It's his deep-sea diving gear.' Eventually the charge was set for hearing in a week's time. Seething, Spargo posted two hundred dollars bail, mustered as much dignity as his pyjamas allowed him, and caught a taxi home.

He found that in his absence his flat had been ransacked. Furniture had been turned over, drawers and book shelves emptied on the floor. All the *Fortuyn* artifacts in the flat had gone.

# 29

On the occasion when I first remember learning something essential about the application of law in sheltered communities I was drinking coffee and eating a sausage roll in the Arcadia Cafe, across the street from the old Perth Police Court, with Tom Gerritty, *The West Australian's* police reporter.

In the court's morning tea break I mentioned to the benignly cynical older journalist that the hearing of the charge against Spargo—of illegally disposing of the ballast brick—had again been adjourned at the Crown's request. This was the fourth or fifth time. Every eight days Spargo would appear in court, the charge would be read, and the police prosecutor would ask the magistrate for another adjournment while the Crown prepared its case.

Gerritty showed no surprise. 'My guess is that they've got no case, but they must be trying to break him. He's a diver, works out of town, has to travel long distances up and down the coastline. It must affect his livelihood to have to appear in court every week.'

'Yes, he's building up a big head of steam.'

It was the first I had heard of the principle of perpetual adjournment. Indefinite postponement is a powerful institutional weapon, but in Spargo it had struck a resistant, and very noisy, adversary.

My memory of this period is as clear as if it were twenty days, not years, ago. I see the police court, its government grey walls, the unsympathetic portrait of the Queen above the magistrate's bench, the heavy jarrah press table on which we scratched our names during boring summons cases against catchers of undersized crayfish and illegal grappa distillers and negligent car drivers. Around this table we also sat alert—a layer of middle-class youthful innocence peeling away with each unfolding of murder, rape and incest evidence, each morning procession of prostitutes, thieves and bashers—and willingly, even gleefully, took our fractured shorthand notes and inhaled crime's toxic odour.

Crime had a sharp smell. It smelled of the urine, sweat, hair oil, blood, vomit and cheap perfume wafting up from the limestone cells below the courts. It smelled of the government floor polish and phenol which caught your nostrils as you climbed the steps from the street. It smelled to us of fundamental and irreparable errors of judgement. The smell of crime wasn't something you could capture in a newspaper paragraph.

Nor could you adequately record the eccentric strand of small-town coincidence which bound people, both participants and observers, together. Officially, the reporter was simply the recorder of events, the objective conduit, but events had a habit of including the messenger in the disorder.

People were always asking you to keep things out of the newspaper: their names, their convictions, their scandals. Bribes were sometimes offered or threats made. But usually they offered you no more than the chance to lessen the indignity they had brought on themselves, and threatened little but the weight of transferred guilt.

Wolf was a case in point. One morning in the crowd milling outside the court room I saw my old mathematics teacher and athletics coach, an aggressive and masculine man in his thirties who had not discouraged the school nickname of 'Wolf'.

Amiably, but with the uneasy deference of the former student, I greeted him, imagining he was in court to answer some traffic charge. He'd always driven his green Vanguard fast and recklessly. He merely grunted and stared expressionlessly ahead of him. Same old Wolf, I thought; as bad-tempered as ever; still over-playing the brusque schoolmaster, the tough sportsman.

But the usual spring was gone from his stride as he climbed the steps into the dock. His offence turned out to be, in the quaint terminology of the charge, 'an act of gross indecency.'

The act had occurred in the front seat of Wolf's Vanguard in the council carpark the night before. A policeman shining his torch into the rocking car had observed that Wolf's penis was in the mouth of a middle-aged insurance salesman.

I took down this evidence in a trance. I could barely look at my former school master, or at the older, pale and nondescript man who also stood in the dock, as far away from Wolf as possible. This was twenty years ago. I was just out of school—and suddenly conscious of many after-sport showers in Wolf's hairy nude company. In retrospect, had he ever acted suspiciously? Not that I remembered. Abruptly my new reporter's sophistication fell away and I felt less than a child, totally naive. What did I know? What was *suspicious* anyway? Until that morning *suspicious* to me had been men with dyed hair and eye-shadow. Suddenly everything was *suspicious*.

Time had flown backward. Now my old headmaster

was peering through the glass doors of the court room as well. But the familiar forbidding eye, the patrician aloofness, had vanished like the spring in Wolf's step. The headmaster was trying to catch my eye as I sat at the press table. I had to remind myself I was wearing my David Jones sports jacket and not a grey school uniform. The headmaster was waggling his fingers at me and there was a weak smile on his face as he beckoned me outside into the corridor.

My instincts were immediately in conflict. Not so long before this man's word had been my command. If he beckoned I jumped. But I knew instantly what he was going to ask, and my proud new journalistic ethics were already bristling self-righteously. I was a professional man now, not a schoolboy, and I had a job to do. I gave the headmaster a firm glance and raised five fingers. I'd see my way clear to join him in five minutes.

Of course when I did meet him outside the court— a deliberate fifteen minutes later—his greeting was unctuous and he beseeched me to 'do something to protect the school's good name.' Wolf's career he dismissed with a curt gesture. He already had his resignation on his desk, he said.

'You'll have to speak to the editor,' I explained. 'It's my job to record every case that appears here.'

He gave me a despairing look and turned on his heel.

He did speak to the editor, and to the managing editor. On a higher level the chairman of the school's board of governors also spoke to the chairman of the newspaper's board of directors. (Several members of the school board were also members of the newspaper board.) However, despite all this activity my story on Wolf's case did appear in next morning's paper.

I wrote only one paragraph. Just the names and addresses and the bare facts of the charges and convictions and $500 fines. There was no special treatment; it was the paper's policy on 'gross indecency' cases not to elaborate on the sordid details. So journalism came through the affair with its honour intact. The disgraced Wolf had to leave the State in order to get another job. And the middle-aged insurance salesman, grossly indecent though married with two grown-up children, killed himself.

———

Yes, events of this time were still clear in my mind twenty years later. This was the time, looking back, when Spargo seemed to me most explicitly himself.

Several months had passed since Sergeant Sikes had charged him with the offence against the Maritime Archeology Act. He must have appeared in court fifteen or sixteen times since, only to have the case adjourned. Now it was early summer, his face was ruddy and damp when he stood in the dock once more to hear the familiar charge read out. The police again asked for an adjournment and the magistrate nodded agreement.

Suddenly Spargo gripped the dock rail and addressed the magistrate. 'Your Honour, it's five months since this charge was laid. I was arrested in embarrassing circumstances and the actual charge is a travesty of justice. I've been forced to appear here every eight days only to repeatedly hear the Crown ask for an adjournment because its case is not prepared.'

The magistrate's eyes widened behind his rimless glasses. The police prosecutor rose to his feet. The court orderlies took a step towards the dock.

'These proceedings are blatantly unfair and unjustified,' Spargo went on. 'If you agree to yet another adjournment I assure you I won't be in court. I have a living to make on the coast and eight days from now I will be on the coast making it.'

The magistrate's face lost its colour, although pink blotches rose around his collar. Leaning forward over his bench, and making an obvious effort to control himself, he said, 'Mister Spargo, you are a prisoner who through the grace of this court is on bail. I am granting the police their adjournment. You will appear here in eight days or face the consequences.'

Spargo said nothing more, but he suddenly looked calmer, at ease with himself once again.

I was in court eight days later when he failed to appear. The magistrate announced, with a significant glance at the press table, that his non-appearance was a blatant contempt of court. He ordered that his bail be forfeited. Then he issued a bench warrant for his arrest.

# 30

The Australian coastline is 17,700 kilometres long. For a year time passed peacefully, with the lines now drawn and precedents firmly established on both sides.

Most of the time Spargo ranged between Darwin and Cairns, humid coastal towns experienced in preserving anonymity. But he made no attempt to hide. The bench warrant wasn't enforceable interstate. He worked under his own name as a salvage diver, then as a seasonal prawn and reef fisherman. He kept in regular contact with Perth.

This is the social network's version. I can't vouch for its accuracy, but at this stage the network was still onside. The network was still supportive enough to remark with general approval how happy Caroline Castle looked when she arrived at lunch with a new letter from somewhere remote and tropical.

It wasn't as if he were the criminal type, the network agreed. Hadn't the police tried something fishy? Hadn't his father or grandfather had a famous old business in the north-west?

The network thought it was romantic—the letters on motel stationery from last-ditch settlements, the multitudinous risks, the whiff of sweat and danger from the East Alligator River and the Arafura Sea.

Apparently very much the *physical* type. Certainly a very *headstrong* boy, this fugitive treasure-hunter of Caroline's. Passions obviously ran deep there. The network even expressed envy. Certain invidious comparisons were made on the domestic front.

The network was aware of the meeting in Darwin.

At short notice she flew recklessly to him. She arrived flustered and distracted by the presence in first-class of an old school dance partner, Tony Blackwood, now one of Peter's lawyers.

'Carly, what on earth are you doing here?' he'd boomed as she crept on board. 'Who ever goes to Darwin?'

'Exactly,' she said.

She feigned tiredness and lay back in her seat with her eyes closed. In Darwin a hot monsoonal rain was falling. She managed to leave the plane last and walked very slowly to the terminal under an airline umbrella. Milky puddles stained her shoes. It smelled almost like Asia but not quite. Not so fecund. Faecal? Rain drummed on metal buildings and slanted against the backs of her legs. In the rain she couldn't feasibly walk any slower to the terminal. And Spargo was standing there, in a T-shirt and shorts, wet-headed, not ten feet from Tony Blackwood, who pretended not to see their difficult kiss. They'd eventually outlasted him over drinks in the bar. When he left they went straight to the Beachcomber Motel for forty-eight hours but she couldn't relax.

The network commiserated. It wondered, however, whether she was being wise. There was the gossip about Tony Blackwood seeing Spargo hoisting her suitcase into the back of a Holden utility at the airport. An old rust-bucket apparently, with drums of petrol or something in the back.

'She looked as furtive as a little skunk,' Tony said.

Of their next planned meeting, therefore, there was

some disapproval and a general readjustment of position. Six months had passed. This time there was plenty of time for her to canvass the pros and cons.

He was working on a prawn trawler out of Weipa, and the trawler's skipper was fascinated by the adventure of investigating in the off-season some of the shipwreck sites Spargo had talked about off Shark Bay. The idea appealed to Spargo, too. For once he'd be able to dive with a big, seaworthy boat at his disposal. There was no risk, he wrote to her; the wrecks were hundreds of miles north of the *Fortuyn* and, anyway, the ballast brick affair had surely blown over. He'd be sailing back into Western Australia for the first time in eighteen months.

'Meet me in Shark Bay in four weeks,' he told her.

The network considered this arrangement. It visualised Spargo's prawn trawler inching bravely around the jagged and lumpy coastline of northern Australia, sailing west and south through the cyclones to the lovers' rendezvous, and it hardened its disapproval. Suddenly the whole thing was getting out of hand. It wasn't an *affair* any longer. It was a romance with a *law-breaker*.

'*Someone* has seen too many movies,' the network concluded, while the more generous members worried aloud about her mental stability and the danger of her 'ruining her life'.

The satisfying phrase, 'for her own good' also began to be bandied about, eventually in delicious conjunction with the even more thrilling words, 'Peter will have to be told.'

# 31

He must have been good in his prime, and feared or loathed, for them to pull out all the stops.

I imagine:

He was tired from the long voyage, the recent diving, and edgy with the anticipation of seeing her. Being together was mysterious. The night they'd met they'd been alone in the party crowd, yet when they were alone together they made a crowded room.

Soon we'll lie on motel sheets without words. Between us only the air of the room, the vacuum we've emptied of all histories, the territory we bring with us.

'I go crazy without you.' First words in the afternoon sun off the sea, dripping wet along the chest and breasts. Swimming like dolphins in the bay, in the water like soft glass. Sliding together, enfolding. His insistent silent question, her cool circling answer. Generously buoyed by the calm swell. Gripped in the sea.

So his mind was on her as the Indian Ocean foamed and settled in the trawler's wake. They were in Shark Bay, five miles from port, when the navy corvette, Acute-class, shot towards them at full steam. It circled the trawler while the sailors on the bridge inspected them through their binoculars, then speeded away towards port.

When the trawler docked it was mid-afternoon. At the jetty there was no Caroline. He waited on board for an hour while the others went to the hotel. Then he joined them. He couldn't miss her, there was no place else to go. There was only one hotel and one motel in town and no booking in either of their names. He drank beer distractedly, pouring schooners down his salty throat, casting his eyes around for her. There were other women in the hotel lounge: busty blonde barmaids, raucous girlfriends of fishermen; their presence mocked her absence.

It grew dark. In the lounge an old man played a piano-accordion and another old man played the spoons and jigged from foot to foot. They played *Danny Boy* and *I Belong to Glasgow* and *Lady of Spain* and a couple of drinkers sang along with the music. In a corner men played darts and from a back room came the smell of frying fish. The cloud of cigarette smoke hanging over the bar was dispersed nearer the door by the cool draught from the sea.

Spargo wearily gathered up his crewmates' empty glasses from their table, took them to the bar and ordered more drinks. With four fresh glasses of beer in his hands he walked back to the table. The breeze from the sea was on his neck. A voice was at his ear.

'Mister Spargo?'

'Yes.'

'I'm placing you under arrest on a bench warrant issued in the Perth Police Court.'

Time froze, and then speeded up. He was turning to the table and towards his crewmates' surprised faces to put the beer glasses down. His torso was twisted towards the table and the glasses were still in his hands when a blow struck the side of his head and he fell across the table in an explosion of liquid and glass.

There was shouting and people rushing in. He was being kicked and hit with truncheons and fists. Beer dripped from the upturned table on to his face. He tried to rise to his feet.

'Get the cuffs on him,' a voice called. 'Don't let the bastard up.'

He stood in a fury and grabbed a constable by the collar and threw him over his hip. Crouching, with a handcuff dangling from one wrist, he faced the police— more than a dozen of them. For some reason the indignity of the single handcuff infuriated him more than the police blows. 'Who put this on me?' he yelled. 'Take it off now!'

Surprisingly one cop stepped forward and removed it. 'You're under arrest, ' he said. 'Just step outside into the car.'

He walked outside into the sea air. As he stepped out of the light he was downed by another rain of blows. He fell to his knees as the boots thudded in. But he grabbed one leg and tilted the kicker over on his back. He kicked groins. He butted heads in a frenzy. He didn't care if he died, and this willing madness telegraphed itself to the police. They stood back and he brushed himself down and walked to the police car.

# PART TWO
# Point-Break

# 1

The summer of 1983-84 was surprisingly easy to recreate. It was so abnormally and relentlessly hot that people readily recalled incidents, dates and the gruelling passage of time.

Strangely, not many people recollected the picture that had stuck in my mind (and, I guessed—in his cell on the other side of the continent—Spargo's mind): that of the dogs hanging themselves.

However, they did recall the cricketers fainting in the field in the Test match against India in December and, for the first time in memory, the absence of seagulls from the cricket ground.

They recalled the trouble one millionaire had in keeping the iceberg presentable for his New Year's Eve *Titanic* party.

They recalled the trouble at Treasure Point in February with the liquefying World War I corpses.

They recalled the heat playing nasty tricks in February with the calibrations of the stringed instruments of the musicians of the London Philharmonic Orchestra who had been transported by another millionaire to play out of doors, in tail-coats, an all-Russian program beginning with Glinka's overture to *Russlan and Ludmilla*.

They recalled—and I saw this for myself when I arrived in late February to try to pin this story down for good—that everywhere the grass was dead and that random fires smoked into the low mauve cloudbank over Treasure Point.

There was no Doctor, no sea-breeze, to disperse the smoky cloud. From time to time there were reports of a sea-breeze, observed out in the ocean and then eagerly anticipated, but this phantom Doctor always mysteriously vanished before it reached the coast. Meanwhile, the Easterly lifted the smoke from the inland bush and swept it over the hot dunes and dropped it in the cloud bank just where the Indian Ocean swell rolled around the point in its pattern of orderly curves. In the sharp crests of this point-break solemn dark-suited figures bobbed on surf boards from dawn till evening. They faced out to sea, squatting on its surface under the bruise-coloured cloud.

Where the point meets the sea here it slopes below the surface into a reef which forms part of a chain of off-shore reefs extending north-south along this section of the coast.

The point and its connecting reefs are part of the same geological formation, created together of Pleistocene eolianite—coastal limestone formed from the dune systems of the Pleistocene epoch—when the sea level was much lower.

The Pleistocene epoch, commonly known as the Ice Age, was characterised by the extensive glaciation of the northern hemisphere and the evolutionary development of man.

History and geography moved slowly here. The point has been named Treasure Point only recently. For more than a hundred years it was known by the settlers and farmers and fishermen as Thirsty Point, perhaps because of the heat-trapping qualities of the natural amphitheatre of limestone and sand dunes which cradles the small bay inside the point. Later, people came naturally to the conclusion that the name referred to the drinking habits of the local crayfishermen.

For thousands of years, however, many centuries before official government policy 'dispersed' them from their traditional fishing grounds, from the area, indeed from the whole south-west coast, the coastal Aborigines knew the point simply as *Yami*—The Place of No Shade.

It was noted by at least one nineteenth century explorer, the intrepid Albert Calvert, author of *The Aborigines of Western Australia, Hints on Gold Prospecting, Pearls: Their Origin and Formation, The Forest Resources of Western Australia* and *Explorations in North-West Australia*, that the physical features of the region closely resembled those of the Holy Land.

'Both suffer from periodical droughts, and largely depend on wells for water; both have fertile and smiling pastures side by side with sandy wastes; both have a warm summer and a pleasant sea breeze near the coast, and both have largely a limestone formation,' Calvert wrote.

'Still more curious to notice is the similarity between the customs of the Aborigines and those of the ancient Jews. The superstitious rites remind us of I Kings, xviii, 28: "And they cried aloud, and cut themselves after their manner with knives and lancets, till the blood gushed out upon them." Then again, Jeremiah xlviii, 37: "For every head shall be bald, and every beard clipped; and upon all the hands shall be cuttings." Here the natives cut off portions of their beards at funerals in addition to lacerating themselves.

'Again in Dueteronomy xviv, 1, it is written, "Ye shall not cut yourselves, nor make any baldness between your eyes, for the dead." Evidently this was an ancient Jewish custom forbidden by Moses. And here we find that when the native females cut and scratch their faces in mourning for the dead, their favourite place for tearing the skin is *between the eyes* as forbidden.'

Of this coast Calvert reported some other Old Testament parallels to his colleagues in the British Explorers' Association. He said that Isaiah, in chapter xlv, verse 4 and 5, could easily have been reprehending the natives for their habit of remaining amongst the graves after funerals. 'And the native form of taking an oath is also very much akin to that described in Genesis xxiv, 9: "And the servant put his head under the thigh of Abraham his master, and sware to him concerning that matter."

'There are the parallels of circumcision, of course. And the native mothers constantly name their children from some circumstance connected with their birth or early infancy, just as in Genesis xxx, 2: "Leah said, A troop cometh, and she called his name Gad."

'It is scarcely necessary,' Calvert concluded, 'that I should disclaim any intention of identifying my Aboriginal friends with the Lost Tribes! I have alluded to the interesting coincidences, but make no attempt to draw inferences therefrom with but meagre data and inadequate knowledge.

'If, however, these primitive people should have received from the Common Creator certain laws for the guidance of their lives, does it not furnish food for reflection?'

Thirsty Point, or *Yami*, may originally have been shadeless, with not a stunted banksia or wind-twisted casuarina to break the glaring line of its moonscape, but its off-shore reefs and lagoons were always fertile with sea-grass and teeming with fish.

During the nineteen-twenties and thirties the crayfishermen who set their pots nearby in the November to April catching season put up a couple of rainwater tanks and a scattering of galvanised iron shacks—and even two bigger iron sheds which they called 'processing factories'—and over the next ten or fifteen years this rusting, ramshackle little settlement slumped quietly in the sand among its broken craypots and pyramid of old beer bottles, known to the outside world, if at all, only for the occasional boating accident and its powerful and intrusive stink in summer.

In World War II the army came up with the idea of using the point for artillery practice. Most of the crayfishermen were away in the services—and they had been illegal squatters anyway—and weren't in a position to complain as live shells flew over, and sometimes into, their shacks.

Forty years after the war, in that summer of unrelieved heat, a rusted tin government notice still warned of the dangers of unexploded shells. *Suspicious objects should not be interfered with, but reported by the quickest means to the nearest police station. DO NOT HANDLE.* Occasionally a weekend gardener or an artesian well digger still turned up a live shell and the army had to be called in to detonate it.

Lying face down in the sand, a bloody bandage round his head, Colonel Tripwire remembered the warning notice and smiled at the idea of a rampaging Turk accidently setting off a shell this afternoon.

# 2

Journalists like to stop time, to pin it down, to mark an X in the air where the bullet stopped. This is both a stylistic and a structural device and allows them to marshal their facts both succinctly and dramatically. It removes the blurry edges of ambiguity and indecision. In this habit they are accentuating the common inclination to remember what one was doing at a particular moment in history, such as when John Lennon was shot.

They are also behaving like embryonic novelists. Ordering time. Playing, just slightly, at being God.

So, let me say that when it was eight p.m. in Sydney, in Long Bay jail, in Spargo's cell in the metropolitan remand centre, on the evening of the day the jury returned to consider its verdict on him and Rosanna, it was still five p.m. at Treasure Point, formerly Thirsty Point, Western Australia.

At five p.m., the colonel recalled, he was lying face down in the sand. At five p.m. the late afternoon sun was still hot enough to melt the corpses' fingers.

Despite the specially chosen later hour the corpses' fingers were causing delays. They wouldn't behave. The fingers were supposed to be contorted expressively in death, to be clawing the air in rigid anguish, but they wouldn't act accordingly.

Some fingers were noticeably moving, slowly curling and uncurling in the sun. Other fingers, of Allies and Turks alike, were actually melting. (Some dummies' noses were similarly liquefying.) One badly mutilated but recalcitrant Turk lay on his back with an arm outstretched and two fingers jabbed defiantly heavenwards. Flushed and damp, a makeup girl darted onto the battlefield and levered out one more digit to ensure the body gave no more than the intended offence.

On the smoky hillside, playing an Australian infantry private, a joke he alone relished, Colonel Tripwire surreptitiously wriggled the toes of his right foot which had gone to sleep.

'You're all dead, guys,' shouted the assistant director. 'Absolutely dead. So don't move.'

The colonel lay absolutely dead and considered this different life.

In America they had all lived such different lives. Obviously he had held public views at the farthest remove from nuclear disarmament and was not a film extra. (Linda had slept with a Smith and Wesson on her bedside table; Leon, presumably, hadn't eaten fresh crayfish three times a week even when it was called rock lobster.)

If violence wasn't a custom here why did he feel he had to be constantly on his mettle?

That morning, after the sixty-first consecutive day in which the Doctor had failed to arrive, he'd risen before dawn to hose his turkeys. Despite his diligence in trying to keep their blood temperature down he had already lost a quarter of his birds to the weather. To make things worse, his sweet potatoes had baked and shrivelled in the ground, his pumpkins boiled to mush inside, the Indian corn—his pride and joy—had borne only fibrous husks.

These failures had disappointed him but, standing

barefoot in the mud of his turkey pen amid the hubbub of the damp and bedraggled survivors, he had just been able to see the prolonged absence of the Doctor as a useful test. It was merely another problem to overcome.

He could cope with landscape; he had beaten landscape. He must remember he'd chosen this particular landscape for its advantages. In this landscape he could escape and evade. Now he must learn to cope with weather. Unremitting extremes in weather were, after all, to be expected in the long, or short, term. Therefore, squirting his turkeys that morning, the colonel had concentrated on weather.

The present weather could be broken down into two factors: wind and heat. The Easterly and the sun. Even before sunrise the Easterly was quickly drying the night's sweat on his scalp and chest. He faced into it. Over the great red tableland and the scrubby escarpment it brought him (personally, he thought) subtle whiffs of gravel dust, eucalypts and dead grasses. When the sun was up the wind delivered him traces of bushfire smoke, hot granite surfaces and something else—a scaly, furry, musty odour that lodged high in his sinuses and reminded him of panicky animals kept in a confined space. Then it scorched and battered his farm, seared his vegetables and sent his turkeys' temperatures soaring.

It was odd remembering how benignly he had regarded the Easterly until the Doctor ceased to arrive. Only the summer before the land and sea breezes had complemented each other. You could set your clock on the Doctor calling at two, bringing relief from the midday heat, and on a calmer, balmy Easterly returning at seven.

His wind chimes always changed tune. When the wind turned around, the brass chimes from Thailand or Kampuchea or wherever changed sound from *tinkle* to *ping*. After their Wednesday tennis game he and Leon would sit on the terrace watching the crayfish boats returning home, laughing at the idea of Flora and Fauna, the crayfish inspectors, spreadeagled in the dunes, spying on the fishermen through their binoculars.

The boats ploughed through the choppy waves. The chimes changed from *tinkle* to *ping*. The smell of backyard barbecues wafted up from Treasure Point. Behind their deck chairs stretched a continent of ancient desert. In front of them the sun sank into the horizon. The glass of beer was cold in the hand; its condensation dampened the palm. How delightful was that first swallow, the prickling in the throat, the hops tangy on the tongue! At these moments there was peace in the soft warm wind and the idea of the land taking over from the sea.

The colonel missed these serene evenings. This summer the heat had stopped their tennis, called a halt to most socialising, especially among the Americans. The last time he had seen them all together had been at the public meeting called after the bombing of the pirate statue.

Maybe it was simply the temperature that had fired up all those old pacifists, that had needled them into applauding this act of community violence. The meeting had touched a nerve. As well as support for Spargo it had brought out into the open the resentment at the recent 'developments'. Most of the speakers had referred to the town, rather belligerently, as Thirsty Point. The Americans in particular had derided the pirate statue and the oceanarium as well as voicing guarded disapproval of the town's change of ownership (Leon had actually moved the motion calling for the charges against Spargo to be dropped and demanding that the council bulldoze the rubble and plant shade trees in the statue's place.)

It encouraged the colonel to see the Americans so resolute. (He'd noted that only a handful of Australians, two South Africans, a Rhodesian and the couple from northern England who ran the Zebra Motel, had bothered to attend—and none of the Chileans or Lebanese.) They had easily defeated the tedious pro-tourism arguments of the motel proprietors, as well as the generalised diatribe from the Australians on the explosion's effect on real estate values.

Usually the Americans' gatherings broke up amid mutual moans about the weather and the unions and vague *sotto voce* complaints of an 'incompleteness'. It seemed to gnaw at them, but they found it hard to be specific about it. It was more and less than homesickness. It was both nationalism denied and it was wry nostalgia. These old liberals could be very difficult: irascible and morally superior one minute, weary and apathetic the next.

After more than twenty years in some cases they were still uncertain immigrants. They were first-stage nuclear refugees, most of them, Cold War pacifists and McCarthy victims hunkered down in the sand dunes nursing their buffalo grass and waiting for their *New Yorkers* and *Atlantics* to arrive three months late.

In their more feisty moments some of them likened Treasure Point to the hills behind Munich, the final retreat—a strange analogy for pacifists, in the colonel's opinion. Others talked restlessly of moving on again, to Tasmania perhaps, or New Zealand.

If he was uneasy with these supposedly kindred spirits, he knew he also made them uneasy. The passionate convert bemused them. Was it his wars they couldn't forgive, or the fact of his one hundred-and-eighty-degree turn? They only rarely turned up for his talks. They gave the impression it was tasteless to preach and argue and cut off all alternatives, to dig in and adapt quite so efficiently to the terrain.

Meanwhile, they kept their sentimental options open by sending away loyally to Brooks Brothers for their cotton shirts and seersucker suits, to L.L. Bean for their sportswear, thus presenting (gravity and increased weight having altered the sizes recorded by their clothiers twenty years before) an awry plaid and buttoned-down image both stereotypically American and climatically unapt.

They mourned their youth too obviously. On Saturday nights they sat on their patios drinking spirits in the heat, playing their Tom Lehrer and Lenny Bruce records and trying not to mind the dearth of invitations from the vice-consulate.

The colonel believed he had discarded fashion, ideology and sentiment. Being someone who had dug a neat hole, dropped his past into it and buried it deep, he could spare them little sympathy.

## 3

The colonel was a story on his own. The colonel was one of the stories I had said I wanted to write so I could write the Spargo story. (To justify to a Sydney or Melbourne editor travelling as far as Perth means promising at least three stories and selling them hard.)

The colonel's real name was Richard W. Magnus but he had attracted much local discussion by laying a network of wires around the perimeter of his property; hence Colonel Tripwire.

His wire was as fine as nylon fishing line and very hard to see nestling at shin level in the dry veldt grass and wild oats. He'd picked up the idea from the Viet Cong. His tripwire was rumoured to be rigged to various booby traps—homemade Claymore mines as big as man-hole covers—but he said that was nonsense. It was just joined to a system of bells and noise-makers fashioned from cans and bottles. He likened it to the little bell a shopkeeper might have on his door to announce customers, or to the rubber tube placed across the driveway of a service station to alert the attendant.

'It's just my early warning device,' Colonel Tripwire told me.

It allowed him to maintain a certain distance, he said.

His 'certain distance', his tripwire, the rumors about the booby traps rigged to it, his awe-inspiring military reputation and, above all, his anti-war stance, had brought a carload of tense detectives up the gravel road to his farm the day after the statue was blown up.

Of course he heard them coming and had some beer out of the fridge and waiting on the verandah long before the police car pulled up.

'Please explain your whereabouts at 1.40 this morning,' they demanded, three stout detectives coming up the steps with their jackets flicked back to show their holsters. They regarded the beer suspiciously. Another man stayed by the car, ostentatiously handling an Armalite.

As it happened the colonel had slept overnight in Margaret River after addressing two hundred people at the Uniting Church hall on 'The Consequences of a Nuclear War for Australia.' He gave the police a leaflet, bold black on yellow, as proof. (*Hear the inside story from a soldier who has fought five wars. Who invaded Kampuchea. Who knows the workings of the Pentagon. Whose chief weapon is now words. His sworn enemy? Nuclear weapons and the Arms Race.*) His audience had included an Independent member of parliament and the district police inspector's mother.

The detectives exchanged looks. That he was probably in the clear seemed to deepen their malaise.

'Kam-pooch-ee-ah?' one sneered.

'Five wars?' queried another. 'You know a few we don't?'

But the colonel's own background enabled him to see the perfect logic in the detectives' mind-set: that the first suspect in a bombing case must be an anti-bomber.

He had been born to soldiering. His opening remarks always electrified his anti-nuclear audiences. 'I was born a patriot in a family of patriots, a hero in a family of heroes. I believed Patrick Henry: "Give me liberty or give me death!" I trembled when I saluted the flag.'

He had devoutly believed his leaders were men of justice and wisdom. He had believed this until 2 April, 1970 when he sat at a trestle table in the village of Muc Hoa on the Vietnam-Cambodia border. Around the table at Muc Hoa his leaders and he had plotted the invasion of Cambodia, and it dawned on him suddenly halfway through their scheming that his leaders weren't men of justice and wisdom any more but just his same old boozing contemporaries. Men like himself.

Men like himself he knew and understood only too well.

The world was a small place when you'd been getting drunk for thirty-five years with the men whose fingers now hovered over the buttons.

Before leaving the Pentagon he'd discovered just how small the world was. The day of his resignation in August 1970 he had used the Pentagon computer to find the safest location in the event of nuclear war. The computer said Australia or New Zealand. The computer further specified a certain box canyon sixty miles from the small town of Te Anau on New Zealand's South Island or a particular valley above Thirsty Point on the edge of the coastal escarpment in south-west Western Australia.

He had been the second officer from Muc Hoa diagnosed as suffering from post-traumatic stress disorder (unresolved grief and unrelieved survivor's guilt with occasional self-destructive impulses) to ask that question of the Pentagon computer. The other colonel had chosen New Zealand.

Colonel Tripwire disagreed with the psychiatrist on the self-destructive impulses. His first priority was to live for as long as possible. For ever. And his grief, if that's what it had been, was now resolved, replaced by another certainty.

Anyway, he preferred warmer weather and a lower population density and so had chosen Australia.

————

On the information provided by the Pentagon computer the colonel could perhaps have predicted Thirsty Point's existing attraction for American nuclear refugees. He couldn't have been expected to predict its metamorphosis into Treasure Point or that a Japanese limestone-and-concrete pirate would eventually rise forty feet from the dunes.

He couldn't even have predicted Peter Castle's original plan for Thirsty Point: to use Spargo's discovery of the *Fortuyn* as the promotional basis for his Treasure Point development.

And he would hardly have guessed at a day like this one, the camera panning across the dusty slope, over the parched grass and buttressed limestone outcrops strewn with newly slaughtered soldiers; the camera sweeping so pruriently over the shell holes and sandbags, over the bloody yellow earth, the severed limbs and smoking devastation, and lingering finally on a limestone ridge where lines of rifles, hammered into the ground barrel-first, stood as grave markers.

The latest World War I film—Treasure Point's first—had created much local curiosity, and pride that the location so resembled the grim cliffs and sandy hillocks of Gallipoli. Many of the townspeople had jobs as extras. When he'd heard that the director wanted to make a passionate anti-war statement, Colonel Tripwire had joined them.

It gave him a peculiar feeling to be lying in the sand playing an anonymous dead man when life had always cast him as the hero. World War I was in fact the only major conflict this century in which he hadn't taken part.

Perhaps that's the reason I'm here, he thought.

The Australians weren't all dead yet. The extras playing the already-dead were allowed to stand up and stretch while one gallant squad of Australians on the perimeter fought on against great odds. Waves of shouting Turks, bayonets fixed, charged towards them.

As the last Australians died bravely the colonel stood and swung his arms to restore circulation. The Easterly blew into his face, drying his sweat and congealing his fake blood. He recognised the manager of the Mobil service station, Con Bournousouzis, bounding down the hill in the front rank of eager Turks. An Australian bullet must have had Con's name on it because he spun abruptly around and hit the ground hard, got to his knees and then collapsed again. Screaming Turks fell dramatically around him.

'Cut! OK, Turks, you're getting melodramatic again,' the director complained. 'Don't die *that* enthusiastically.'

The director had a commitment to realism. When enough Australians and Turks were dead to satisfy him, and in the right proportion to achieve symmetry, the crew began to shoot a scene in which several rats had to crawl across some corpses in a trench. But the rats refused to crawl over the bodies.

'Come on you little bastards,' the assistant director coaxed.

The rats wouldn't respond. They were disdainful and hygienic, bred for cool laboratories, and not used to the bright, loud and distasteful outdoors.

'Get them to crawl for Christ's sake,' the director

shouted at the rats' handler. The crew began to titter. The rats' handler said they were suffering from heat exhaustion. It was decided to carry them into the director's air-conditioned trailer to recover. The scene was postponed.

'OK, lie down again, please guys,' yelled the assistant director to the extras playing dead soldiers. 'And get those sunglasses off!'

The colonel adjusted his head bandage and lay on his face again, dead in the sun, trying to ally this mock war to the Pacific and Korea and Indo-China. In Korea he'd also been shot in the head and had refused to leave the battlefield. When his C.O. crawled over to tell him he'd been promoted to captain the blood was frozen around his head in a helmet of ice. He never even lost consciousness.

His cheek rested against the butt of his Lee-Enfield .303, like the others on the battlefield borrowed from a high school cadet corps. He couldn't remember ever firing one of these old rifles, even at West Point, and for a second he wished it were loaded. He had metal in his body from three wars and he'd never passed out once. He wondered why not. This sensation of enforced passivity wasn't entirely unpleasant, despite the temperature. Furry spots swam in his half-closed eyes.

The sun was the other factor of the weather he must consider. In this clear sky the sunlight was extraordinary, blinding, once it rose high and struck the dunes. The local people's faces wrinkled constantly against the glare. This painful clarity, its lack of filters, affected behaviour. It could induce nausea, its subliminal flickers even causing spasms like epilepsy in the unwary, unshaded foreigner.

He never went out without a wide-brimmed hat. He believed it was the light which prevented nuances and ambiguity in this country. He couldn't see any subtle shades of grey. Everyone was amiable or an enemy.

The sun here was a wonder. When he'd finished watering his turkeys that morning he'd watched it rising inexorably over the escarpment into his valley, for the sixty-second consecutive day without a sea-breeze, and yet at its appearance the birds shook their wattles, spread their tails and looked alert and optimistic. He'd caught the mood of the bright dawn. His generators were, after all, humming. His tanks were at least full of bore water. His citrus trees, figs, guavas, olives and almonds were hanging on.

His mouth tasted of figs and he felt on top of things again.

Even the small victories counted. In the breath of the Easterly, concentrating hard, testing himself, he thought he'd detected the scratchy tracks of reptiles and marsupials, the saline sourness of erosion and the gritty remnants of ghost-gum bark. He bent down and picked up a pellet from his potato bed. Sheep? No, it would have tripped the wire. Kangaroo? Possum?

He broke the pellet in half and sniffed. Rabbit, he announced to himself with satisfaction, and set new traps around the vegetables.

Lying dead now, he remembered the reluctant rats, and smiled into the sand. Tomorrow, he'd heard, the director's commitment to realism would go so far as to use maggots on some of the corpses. The smoke of the battlefield wafted over him and his fellow corpses and rose into the late afternoon sky. The crew was burning incense to simulate the smoke of warfare.

The Easterly took the incense smoke and blew it down the hillside and over the point, where it gathered in the mauve cloudbank. This was very different to all his other wars. World War I smelled like a church.

# 4

To blow up the pirate statue (was it meant to be Blackbeard? Captain Kidd?) someone had packed six sticks of gelignite into a bed of fertiliser soaked in dieseline—a trick used by some farmers to increase the blast when blowing up big tree stumps—and jammed the bomb into a crevice between the pirate's boot heels.

In the middle of the night the explosion, detonated by a fifty-metre fuse, woke people all over town. The main force of the explosion travelled upwards and literally blew Blackbeard out of his sea-boots. His limestone components crumpled into powder and his concrete portions scattered over several acres. Sand and fertiliser rained over Treasure Point.

It was the effectiveness of the blast which turned the detectives' attention to Spargo. By then everyone was mentioning his name in any case. Wasn't he a 'six-stick man'? Wasn't he jaundiced by events? Didn't he have an axe to grind?

Not so, he said at his trial, the statue-bombing trial in May 1980. There were a lot of questions hanging in the air by then. The defence found it necessary to detail the changes to Thirsty Point since the *Fortuyn's* discovery. Not only did the crayfishermen's huts and the bottle heap bring a nostalgic smile to the jury's lips, but an uncharacteristic picture of Peter Castle emerged.

His only business failure was laid before the court. Of course, he agreed, the Castle Group had planned to develop the two thousand acres of sand dunes and pigface to capitalise on Spargo's discovery. He agreed that he had brought in the Shindai Corporation of Japan as a forty-nine per cent partner in his original Treasure Point development.

His plan had been to sell one thousand suburban blocks a year. He had envisaged Treasure Point's eventual population at two hundred thousand. Yes, ten years later he had, unfortunately sold only two thousand blocks and property values had actually fallen in a boom market.

He had looked everywhere for land buyers. With a conservative government's assistance he had recruited white Rhodesians and South Africans as settlers. When the government changed he had turned his attention to Chile and Lebanon.

'Only middle-class professionals,' he stressed. 'No trouble-makers.'

It was with relief, he admitted, that he had finally managed to sell Shindai his fifty-one per cent of Treasure Point for ten million dollars plus the project's accumulated debts of thirty-five million dollars.

Spargo's counsel spoke very slowly. 'So, Mr Castle, you sold an Australian town, a West Australian community, holus-bolus to the Japanese?'

'Yes, if you want to be xenophobic about it.'

If Spargo's counsel was pitching to the nationalistic juror, the World War II veteran, he was on shaky ground. The prosecution had automatically eliminated every potential juror over fifty.

'And some citizen—not my client—in breach of the

law, certainly—some citizen was moved to harmlessly protest this action?'

'Well, someone was moved to bomb the statue, that's for sure.'

'A purely symbolic action, wouldn't you say?'

'I wouldn't know. Symbolism isn't my strong point.'

It was clear that his strong point was unloading business failures on to foreigners.

To open, as I do now, a copy of the Treasure Point *Advocate* and see the party photographs of gregarious Australian males roistering at their cricket club socials (many of them actually former Rhodesians; they seemed to adapt most readily to the local drinking and sporting customs), one would never imagine the town was owned by the Japanese. Nor that it was an artifice created by one company and sold to another. There is not an Asian face in the newspaper.

At the time of the takeover of the town the *Business Review Weekly* described Shindai as a 'vast entertainment conglomerate with a turnover of billions of dollars a year'. It seemed that Shindai knew the tourist industry and tourists these days wanted dolphins and aquatic playgrounds. So Shindai built an oceanarium and staffed it with killer-whale curators and sea-lion trainers, aquarists, marine veterinarians and vivacious blonde dolphin communicators.

Shindai came up with the idea of a pirate captain as the symbol of the town, the logotype for its promotional material, and erected a statue of this unnamed pirate on the highest sandhill overlooking the town.

Towards the end of the statue-bombing trial the defence produced a professor of Japanese and asked him what *shindai* meant. He said that *shindai* was the traditional word for bed.

'Not just the bed itself but everything to do with bed.'

The eyes of the defence counsel sparkled. 'Of course the town is not owned by a porno company?'

'Of course not. I believe that *shindai* also means the traditional art of pillow-fighting, which in Japan is an intimate physical and romantic ritual between men and women.'

The jury's eyebrows raised.

My copy of the *Advocate*—15 May, 1980—has a page one picture of Spargo. He is wearing a suit and tie and shows the first signs of physical vulnerability. An arm of his reading glasses protrudes from his jacket pocket. His hair is receding. Otherwise he is as ruddy and robust as ever, smiling and shaking hands with his counsel outside the Supreme Court after his acquittal.

Like many photographs this one is as interesting for its background, its supporting actors, as it is for its subject. Two frowning men, from their physiques and suits obviously police, are coming down the steps behind Spargo and the lawyer. Their expressions speak for them, and their contours, even slightly out of focus, are as inevitable as landmarks.

# 5

Like Colonel Tripwire there was one American couple, named Lawson, who had arrived in Treasure Point much later than the Cold War pacifists. The Lawsons had emigrated—from New York, they said—in 1979.

After several weeks settling into the town and investigating business opportunities they had opened a shop in Mermaid Mall selling screen-printed T-shirts. It was a surprisingly simple and lucrative business with few overheads. They bought cotton and cotton-polyester T-shirts from the wholesalers for between three and five dollars each—depending on the quality and the fabric mix—and sold them, screen-printed in one colour, for between ten and fifteen dollars each.

Lawson had absorbed himself in the preparations for the business. He made the wooden printing frames himself and fixed the silk mesh across them. Although he could have bought them at the hardware shop, he even made the squeegees—the short strips of wood with hard rubber along one edge—with which he pressed the pigment through a stencil over the mesh and on to the shirts.

The artwork was also his own. He designed the stencils around a few basic themes—a treasure chest, a pirate's face, a coconut palm, a crayfish, a sailboard—arranged in artistic conjunction with the words 'Treasure Point'.

The business could not have been much easier to operate. This was important because Mrs Lawson was bound to a wheelchair and tired easily. Lawson printed the 'garments' (as they learned, in the jargon of the clothing industry, to call them) in the back room. His wife sat in her chair behind the cash register. They employed a local girl to serve the customers and attend to the racks of T-shirts in the front of the shop.

While it was a seasonal business, with summer their busiest period, they were fortunately not dependent on the tourist market. The T-shirt was the uniform of Treasure Point. The aquarists at the oceanarium, the waiters and waitresses at the Buccaneer and Davy Jones and Lobster Pot restaurants, the barmaids at Moby Dick's Tavern, the sporting clubs, the children of both the Treasure Point State School and the Star of the Sea Convent all soon wore T-shirts whose designs and emblems had been drawn and crafted by Leon Lawson.

In the beginning it amused him to see some tubby young matron flaunting one of his crayfish or treasure chests across her bosom. It had also been a joke, after the statue-bombing incident, to caricature Spargo's face for his pirate stencil. The joke had since worn very thin.

In hot weather he and his wife wore their 'garments' themselves. However, they chose plain cotton shirts with no exhibitionistic crayfish or pirates. They had no wish to draw unnecessary attention to themselves.

Lately he had drawn attention to himself—by moving the resolution at the public meeting on the bombed statue, by going to Sydney to give evidence at Spargo's conspiracy-to-murder trial.

Unlike Colonel Tripwire he was worried about becoming 'known'.

# 6

You are naturally wondering about this second Lawson. The question of two unrelated characters with the same name is almost too confusing to contemplate. This is certainly the case in fiction. In real life, however, even in journalism, relatively common names like Lawson abound. So do coincidences for that matter.

In real life, on the evening of 16 February, 1984, while the jury was out deciding the fate of Spargo and Rosanna, this second Lawson admitted to me that he had actually changed his name to Lawson. To my question he answered tersely that, no, he couldn't remember ever hearing of Len Lawson, the cartoonist-rapist-murderer, alias the Lone Avenger, and, as he said, 'Why would I choose the name of such a person anyway?'

But subconsciously? When he had last been in Australia, in 1962-63, Len Lawson had been much in the news for murdering the 'churchgoing' girl, for holding the girls' boarding-school to ransom and then murdering the fifteen-year-old schoolgirl. And there was the coincidence of them both being cartoonists.

I wondered whether the ricochet principle could work subconsciously.

This Lawson told me, rather self-consciously and defensively, that the name had come to him as a minor variation on his real name. It was merely an Anglicising, an Australianising, of his real name.

'My name means a lot to me and I didn't want to change it drastically,' he said.

Of course this second Lawson was the former Leon Levinson whom I had interviewed so exhaustively in the Esplanade Hotel in Perth more than twenty years before. During the trial I had heard the court orderly call, 'Leon Lawson!' and seen this vaguely familiar man stride through the court and into the witness box. However, I couldn't place him. Then when I heard his accent as he was sworn in I remembered him and thought the orderly had mispronounced his name. But to the defence counsel's opening question, 'Are you Leon Lawson?' he answered, 'I am.'

Five minutes later, after he had been asked to stand down, he seemed surprised when in the corridor outside the court I called out, 'Mr. Levinson!' But he couldn't prevent himself half turning and giving me an embarrassed glance before hurrying out of the building.

He was in court again next day, however, looking wary and unhappy as the prosecution and defence summed up their cases. When the jury retired I hurried over, intensely curious, and introduced myself, mentioning our meeting in the sixties. He nodded, tense, but, recovering quickly, agreed to a drink and suggested the Sheraton Wentworth Hotel nearby.

Apologising for hurrying away the day before, he said the past few days had made him nervy and restless. He was now anxious about the verdict expected tonight or tomorrow, and at the same time frustrated that he couldn't have been more helpful to the defence.

'A week ago I couldn't have imagined feeling this way,' he said. 'I was furious when the subpoena arrived from

Spargo's solicitors to give evidence for him. The gall!
"It's not possible," I thought. "What can I say in his
favour, even if I wanted to?"'

But he had grudgingly travelled east, booked into the
Sheraton Wentworth to be near the District Court, and
turned up at 10 a.m. on the appointed day.

Late that afternoon he had at last been called to the
witness box. He got no further than the swearing-in and
stating his name before the prosecution mysteriously but
successfully disputed his appearance and the judge asked
him to stand down. As he left the box, bewildered, Spargo
had caught his eye and winked. Two detectives sitting
in the front row of the public gallery had seen this brief
play of features, nudged each other and followed the
remainder of his progress through the court with their
eyes.

He had decided to stay until the end of the trial.

'I can still feel the detectives' eyes on my back,' he
told me.

Now he felt 'known' in Sydney, too.

———————

That evening we drank steadily while waiting for the
jury to return. By seven, when the jury called for dinner,
it became clear they would be locked in for the night.
We had a meal ourselves, and more drinks. While much
changed from the ebullient fellow I had interviewed in
Perth, Lawson gradually became more relaxed and expansive with alcohol, although what he said at first made
sense only intermittently.

'Why change your name?' I asked as soon as it was
possible.

'A form of escape,' he said. Then he retreated into
philosophising, avoiding the subject. 'I look back on

my escapes. Why am I always escaping?' He shrugged his shoulders. He supposed he had always been a 'rootless cosmopolitan—that derogatory term beloved of Soviet Russia'. He could hardly deny it, he said with a brittle laugh. He had escaped from Budapest to Pisa, from Pisa to New York, from New York to San Francisco, from San Francisco to Treasure Point.

As if it had just occurred to him, he said thoughtfully, 'Surely it must be some sort of bizarre record that I have escaped from both Europe *and* America.'

'And now? What are you doing in Australia?'

'Again I have escaped the decision about who and what I am.'

By this stage an unreal and suspenseful cloud hung over the evening. Drink was flowing. The jury was out. Decisions were in tense abeyance. The bullet hung motionless in the dusty air.

'So?' I asked harshly. 'Who and what are you? Why not make the decision now?'

'A split personality,' he said.

———

By 1941 he was already a split personality: a cocky young cartoonist and an anxious would-be architect. That year *Life* had published some of his drawings while he was still at the Politecnico in Pisa. It was regarded as a coup for a cartoonist, especially a European one, to elbow his way into the magazine between all those stark war photographs by Margaret Bourke-White and Robert Capa.

*Life* was the big time, even if the general standard of American black-and-white art was derided by Europeans. All those *Saturday Evening Post* gags of desert islands and fat cannibals in chefs' hats! To the Poli-

tecnico's student sophisticates they were insipid and bour-
geois, content with the easy laugh. And the political
cartoons were even worse, as grey and declamatory as
provincial editorials.

The trouble was that the Americans were uneasy with
satire. They had no irony. Their pens were never needles.
Later, as an American himself, he appreciated an exception to this banality and bombast—the comic strip. This
was where they shone.

If he had learned nothing else from America he had
discovered that life imitates not art so much as the comic
strip.

His cartoons were seen as a curiosity. His first drawings
for *Life*, published as *Italian Sketchbook*, showed
*carabinieri* strutting around the Leaning Tower, *fascisti*
saluting each other in the Piazza San Marco, army
goose-steppers parading past the Coliseum. He drew the
familiar classic architectural wonders looming large
behind and around these tiny, self-important figures. He
was heavy-handed (and also light-handed) in his depic-
tion of human frailty. The strong continuous line showed
the grandeur of the buildings. The people were all
stippled figures. Men of dots.

He heard later that the issue was banned in Italy, but
by the time it was published he was in Lisbon with
an imaginatively designed passport. He sailed in the
*Maximilian* to Ellis Island and a year later was an American citizen.

At Ellis Island United States Immigration gave him
a present, a new middle initial. He had only one given
name, Leon, and this unsettled them. The Americans
liked a middle initial. He took J, for Jacob, for his father.

Now he had jettisoned his family name. The J was
all he had of him.

But every morning when he put on his socks at the

other end of the world he thought of his father. He had been a manufacturer of socks and underwear in Budapest. He marketed his garments under the label of a swan. Swan-brand socks and Swan-brand vests had made for a cosy upbringing.

Maybe that was why Western Australia had such a hold on him. The swan was its state emblem. Maybe this was also why he drank so much of the local beer, Swan Lager. The beer had a swan on the label too, like his father's socks and vests. Not a white swan this time, but a black swan. This was the land of contraries.

# 7

Strangely, what the then Leon Levinson had begun to regard as his gutlessness back in the forties, his lack of decision, was seen by the critics as Art. Unintentionally he had them tantalised.

After his first exhibition one of the important New York critics had burst into print: 'It is impossible to pigeon-hole Leon Levinson. Is he a writer of drawings? An architect of satire? A draftsman of psychological and philosophical reflections? The answer is Yes. Levinson is all these things—and more.'

Levinson couldn't say he wasn't grateful for that sort of notice, any notice, in 1948. It did him good, but it harmed him, too. It kept him irresolute longer.

Another important critic went right out on a limb: 'His cartoon-monologues create pictures which are words, and words which have the tangibility of objects. The result is a novel form of art.' And then this man boldly asserted: 'Despite the deceptive simplicity of his images, their intellectual complexities and the fact that he is drawn to pen and ink mark Levinson as a new and intriguing kind of *writer*.'

There it was. But he wouldn't take the hint.

The trouble with this puzzled but generous reception

was that it brought home to him the slippery advantage of being a borderline artist. It allowed him the luxury of putting off indefinitely what he wanted to be.

He felt he had hedged his way through the fifties, the Cold War, the McCarthy purges, as lives and reputations fell into shreds around him. He had escaped the tentacles by keeping moving, nudged along by politics, wars and travel for travel's sake.

He saw now that his line was a fine one.

As the sixties began he became less and less happy at the idea of being involved in aesthetics alone. It was important to say something. By the mid-sixties events began to force the issue. In Saigon in 1967 he grew suddenly tired of making ironic drawings of Marshal Ky's silk scarf and pearl-handled revolvers. Even in 1967 Vietnam was beyond irony.

Like many other war observers he was frustrated by his limitations. More than ever people and events were becoming indistinguishable from the fabricated versions of them distributed to and by the media. Nothing was real until it was reproduced.

Believing that only the war photographers and TV cameramen could repaint *Guernica*, he spent weeks disposing of his *Life* expenses in low dives with teenage prostitutes, CIA observers and French wire-service men. He had a pistol, too, and a couple of drip-dry, military-style, jungle-green shirts, like all the other noncombatants, with epaulettes and dinky pockets on the sleeves to hold his Camels, but they didn't protect him against Saigon Rose or even Chivas Regal hangovers.

Drawing was his way of reasoning on paper, and he could no longer extract any reason from the events around him. The real subjects were elusive. What were they? He wondered whether his talent was faulty. He became more political. He even played around with his style, jettisoning his continuous line and inventing a chaotic skew-line which he thought better suited to detailing the anxieties of modern life and politics. *Life* didn't like it, and neither did he. No offence to Hogarth and Daumier, but these were times too devious and subtle for the savage lithograph. And his new skew-line treatment of politics put *him* into the picture, too. He wanted to keep his distance.

In the end he fell back on his architectural training, trying once again to eliminate his natural clumsiness, his ready-made vocabulary. Again he drew from life, *dal vero*.

This more representational mode retained enough of his old trademarks to keep everyone happy. *Life* liked the softened political approach and the swing back to buildings, landscape, crowds, cafes, the full picture. So did everyone. In China, entering with Nixon's party, Levinson drew 'from the true' and it worked so well that Pat Nixon requested his original drawings for the wall of the family room at San Clemente.

He believed he was at his lowest ebb.

And then *Life* ended.

# 8

The closing of *Life* in 1972 was like the death of a parent in young middle-age. It was an immense blow to Levinson. He couldn't understand it. His system couldn't take it.

For thirty of its thirty-six years *Life* had kept him busy being a new American, dancing between art and journalism, dashing around the country and the world in a state of high stimulation.

Most immigrants nestled in somewhere where they could feel secure. *Life* and he had been happier for him not to put down roots. Being an immigrant was a state he actually preferred. It gave him official spectator status. He arrived in New York only to keep moving.

In the beginning he'd kept two rooms as a base in Bleecker Street, above a pasta restaurant. After his Italian student years he needed the food, although Sam's didn't run to Pisan cooking, Bianco Pisano di San Torpè or even rough Tuscan chianti. On his first night, inquiring in his Tuscan accent after *cèe*, baby eels cooked in olive oil, garlic and sage, he went close to making a foe for life. Luckily Sam made allowances for creative types. Three other Calabrians had been machine-gunned on the premises under earlier management, and this made the place a favourite with the arty set.

At this time, 1942—when he was in town—he lived with Elizabeth Lasker during the week in Bleecker Street. She was a publisher's editor with a husband in Bennington, Vermont. On Fridays he would see her off at the Greyhound terminal. While she returned to her marriage he would party and play the bohemian.

But *Life* and he wanted him to travel. By train and bus he investigated America, sketching as he went. This was before tinted windows when the view from a high Greyhound was better than that from a car. A car was too close to the road and threatened by other machinery; the train and bus were aloof from the tensions of street level. He could sit back and take in the full picture. On the street was public America; above the street were the private lives.

Above the street a dentist pulled teeth in Albany, New York. Above the street an accountant paced nervously in Redding, California. There was a draft board medical in San Diego, a smiling mulatto prostitute disrobing in New Orleans. Above the street were grandmothers, babies and birds in cages. Men in vests smoked cigarettes and stared out the windows of rooming houses and waited to enter the war.

The Greyhound was an education. Outside Memphis he was punched on the ear by a drunken G.I.—sitting seething behind him—who took his accent for German! And on the walls of bus station latrines he learned much more than the American vernacular. In his enthusiasm he saw the lavatory-wall scrawl as art taken right back to its essence. It went back beyond naive art and the drawings of children and the mentally disturbed and the cave drawings of pre-history. Back to Day One.

*Life* was now his country and he obeyed its call.

He went to war for *Life*. He was attached to the Fifth Army. As far as he had any choice in the matter, he chose Italy for his war. This was part nostalgia, part cowardice. He had been lulled by Mussolini's resignation and then by Italy's surrender into imagining the landing at Salerno would be a breeze. He was wrong.

He soon found there were drawbacks in representing *Life*. *Life* was America. In the matter of publicity Clark was no MacArthur, or even a Patton, but the general still wanted the men from *Life* and *Time* and *The New York Times* up there reporting and photographing and drawing him winning battles.

At Salerno Levinson was surprised to find his role so precisely defined. He was a war artist, a symbol. Of course, the British did this sort of thing so much better. One of their divisions had a man from the Royal Academy who lit up his pipe, set up his easel on the deck of his destroyer, mixed his oils and painted away while the shells flew over his head. Under fire, Levinson could barely draw a stick figure. He would have welcomed the periphery, but the man from *Life* had to *be there*.

So as the man from *Life* he entered Naples with the liberating advance troops on 1 October, 1943. He had no say in it. No journalistic acumen was involved. Courtesy of General Clark he had a jeep and a corporal-driver from Amarillo, Texas. Laughing, weeping Neapolitans embraced him, threw blossoms and pressed crucifixes on him. Imposters, too, could be moved to tears. He handed out chocolate with the best of them.

The Germans had retreated to Vesuvius. What a chance for God here! Levinson willed the volcano to erupt and turn them into Pompeiian pumice. What perfect statues they would make, what neat and well-defined fossils! But as usual there was no Old Testament symmetry, no appreciation of aptness. Instead, Vesuvius charged the Germans' batteries.

The Germans fought back fiercely as the Fifth Army advanced north towards the Volturno River, hampered by demolitions, mines and swollen mountain torrents. The Americans and British crossed the river in every type of makeshift craft. Levinson shared a purloined punt with the *Herald-Tribune*. It capsized after a few yards and they were thrown into the water. Swimming across the Volturno under mortar fire and intermittent machine-gun bursts, trying to keep his satchel of materials dry, he felt himself for the first time to be a real war correspondent, blooded at last.

Shortly after, he completed his first drawing of the Italian campaign. He sketched an American gun position on a terrace in the ornately fountained garden of King Victor Emmanuel's palace at Caserta. The barrel of a 155mm howitzer protruded over a marble parapet. Exhausted artillerymen squatted on sandbags, or leaned, smoking, against statues of angels. Although most essential services had been blown up by the departing Germans, the seraphim, mysteriously, still spurted water.

His perspective was a little shaky but he was pleased with the seraphim.

And then *Life* abruptly decided that Italy was slow going. It could be months before the Fifth and Eighth armies broke through to Pisa and Florence. As usual *Life* wanted the full picture. *Life* wanted the Far East. Levinson was transferred to Burma.

In Burma his chosen role as spectator was never more pronounced. The war there seemed even further removed from America. Tagging along with the British and Indian troops of the 14th Army he found himself filling pages with hackneyed cartoons of skinny rickshaw boys hauling ruddy-faced colonels.

He successfully submitted a drawing of a party of Royal Scots Fusiliers playing the bagpipes as they stamped through a boggy tributary of the Irrawaddy. (Had he been a Japanese sniper he would have found no target more irresistible.)

He unsuccessfully submitted a drawing of the celebrations of the liberation of Rangoon. (His taste and judgment were weakened by hangovers and malaria.) His sketch showed a Welsh infantry sergeant winning the contest for urinating on the most geckoes on the wall of the men's room of the Aladdin nightclub. (The sergeant's score was twelve.)

At the end, especially at the end, *Life* was there. Aboard the *Missouri* MacArthur's staff demanded a drawing of the final ceremony. He made two sketches of the Japanese diplomats in their frock coats and top hats signing the document of surrender. The drawing he signed and gave MacArthur was strictly the more accurate, *dal vero*. With the drawing intended for publication he fudged a little for reasons of taste and charity.

Like the seraphim at Victor Emmanuel's palace and the Welsh infantry sergeant in Rangoon, the Japanese foreign secretary, Shigemitsu, was not fazed by the big event. He was able to perform under pressure, indeed found it impossible not to do so. However, the drawing which made the cover of *Life* showed as shadow the small puddle on the deck.

# 9

At least the passing of *Life* made one decision for him. Now he had the chance to bite the bullet. To opt for art, completely and unreservedly. But still he wavered. After thirty years he was used to being on the move constantly, getting good money and having a foot in each camp. Without the jagged contrapuntal melodies of commerce, travel and occasional physical risk would he even have any music to play? Why did he have to choose a category anyway? What was the matter with being a borderline artist?

He agonised that he had never tested his solitude or the courage of any single action. Could now be the time to do so? For more than a month he sat tight in his New York apartment, rarely venturing outside, ostensibly selecting work from his China trip for exhibition, but feeling increasingly trapped by this enforced freedom, encircled by his continuous line.

It was an historical quandary. Who had ever handled it properly; to be honest—without qualms? Leonardo? Even Leonardo was defensive. Leonardo's ability in many art forms had led him to compare what they had in common and where they differed, and this had strengthened his defence of painting over everything else. But then Leonardo had always smarted at the prevailing scholastic classification of poetry and music as among the highest forms of human effort, while the academics relegated painting to the 'mechanical arts', to arts and crafts. Down there with sculpture and dish-making.

Leonardo grudgingly gave music a few points as 'the sister of painting', for being dependent on hearing— the second sense—and for having harmony (like painting, composed of the union of its proportional parts exerting their influence simultaneously). 'Unfortunately,' Leonardo sniffed, 'it fades away as soon as it is born.' Unlike painting.

And as for writing! There was as much similarity between the poet's and the painter's representation of the human figure as there was between a dismembered and a whole body. The poet could only show you beauty or ugliness consecutively, bit by bit, whereas the painter could display it all at once.

Leonardo went further (at the same time, with much irony and some false humility, referring to himself as an *uomo senza lettere*): 'If poetry treats of moral philosophy, painting has to with natural philosophy. If poetry describes the working of the mind, painting considers the working of the mind as reflected in the movements of the body.

'If poetry can terrify people by fictions of hell, painting can do as much by placing the same things before the eye. (*So long, Dante.*) Suppose the poet is set against the painter to represent beauty, terror or a base, ugly, monstrous thing; whatever the forms he may in his way produce, the painter will satisfy the more. Have we not seen pictures so closely resembling the actual thing that they have deceived both men and beasts?'

It made things very difficult. Levinson had fallen back on Leonardo's advice ever since Pisa and his architectural studies at the Politecnico, when Leonardo's views had formed the basis of his very first lesson:

## What is an arch?

An arch is nothing else than a strength caused by two weaknesses; for the arch in a building is made up of two segments of a circle, and each of these segments being in itself very weak desires to fall, and as one withstands the downfall of the other the two weaknesses are converted into a single strength.

Levinson's own strength was his weakness, however. His strength was his line and the line was only an adolescent stage in the science and geometry of art, just above the meagre and barely existent point.

'*Let no man who is not a mathematician read the elements of my work,*' Leonardo ordered. Thundered. But Levinson was looking for omens and wouldn't be put off. Anyway, he had his own rigid training. *Dal vero.*

A point is that which has no centre. It has neither breadth, length nor depth. *A line is a length produced by the movement of a point, and its extremities are points. It has neither breadth nor depth.* A surface is an extension made by the transversal movement of a line, and its extremities are lines. (A surface has no depth.) A body is a quantity formed by the lateral movement of a surface and its boundaries are surfaces. A body has length and breadth and depth.

———

For a month Levinson saw no-one, went to no parties. An answering service gathered all his phone calls. His mail went unanswered. Among both the calls and letters were several offers of pleasant and lucrative work to which he did not reply. The forthcoming exhibition (tentatively entitled *Travel*), for which he had committed work from his China trip, was scheduled for next month but he couldn't bring himself to make a selection from his drawings.

———————

Leonardo:

1. The surface is a limitation of the body.
2. The limitation of the body is no part of that body.
3. That which is not part of any body is a thing of naught.
4. A thing of naught is that which fills no space. The limitation of one body is that which begins another.

The boundary of one thing with another is of the nature of a mathematical line, but not of a drawn line because the end of one colour is the beginning of another colour—the boundary is a thing invisible.

Empty space begins where the object ends. Where empty space ends the object begins and where the object ends emptiness begins.

———————

What had fascinated him in China was not the politics ('This is a great Wall!'—Richard Nixon), not the expected famous sights and sensations: the crowds, the cacophony of official greetings, gongs, drums, streamers and bicycle bells, but the unexpected ironies. To be stared at in Urumchi, the capital of the Sinkiang Uighur Autonomous Region, by green eyes in white-skinned faces. To watch, at Lake Tien Ch'ih, high in the Tien-shan Mountains, green-eyed, brightly-costumed, heavily rouged women, gyrating their bare bellies in a local version of the Dance of the Seven Veils.

All turned on by the Information Department, of course, its Peking officials all chain-smoking nervily like country boys at a strip show, eyes riveted on the women's bodies, muttering sly, deadpan cracks to each other, gathering in tight groups and relaxing only enough to clap lightly at the end of the performance.

He drew department stores (first floor—bicycle seats, second floor—vacuum flasks, third floor—saucepans). He drew the crack Third Division of the People's Liberation Army displaying their skills at short-range anti-paratrooper rocket fire. (He drew Nixon sipping orange-ade under a Mao portrait, just for the record.) And he drew the people of Sinkiang: the curious Uighur, Kazakh, Kirghiz, Klualka, Tadjik, Mongol, Hui, Uzbek and Tartar faces which were fast being absorbed in the great Han melting pot. Drew them quickly before Peking trucked in another two or three million Han families as a human buffer against Russia and India. Shy faces from ancient history; polite and smiling dying races.

He drew their line too—while it lasted. Peking was forcibly replacing the Arabic scripts of their Uighur and Kazakh languages with a romanised phonetic script which the Han could understand. So he took their line and set it down.

---

The point has no centre but is itself a centre and nothing can be smaller. The point is the minimum. The point is indivisible by the mind. The point has no parts. The point is the end which nothingness and the line have in common. It is neither nothingness nor line, nor does it occupy a space between them. Therefore the end of nothingness and the beginning of the line are in contact with one another, but they are not joined together for between them, dividing them, is the point...

And from this it follows that many points imagined in continuous contact do not constitute the line and therefore many lines in continuous contact along their sides do not make a surface, nor do many surfaces in continuous contact make a body, because among us bodies are not formed of incorporeal things...

Not for the last time Levinson considered that life was like a sketch. No, 'sketch' wasn't quite the word, because a sketch was an outline of something, the basis for a picture, whereas the sketch that was our life was a sketch for nothing, an outline with no picture.

The perfect example of an outline was of course the coastline. Life was like a coastline, of widely differing physical features—from steep fiords to sheltered bays and benign flat sandy stretches—which while serving as the perimeter of possibilities also gave no hint as to what lay within.

# 10

There were no hints the night of the Nicaraguan film party in San Francisco of what lay inland. Or perhaps he had just ignored them: her presentation, her intensity, her effect on people.

The track into the interior, however, had been surprisingly easy going. Next morning he'd rung her office and invited her to his exhibition at the de Young Museum.

'When?' she asked.

'How about now?'

'One hour.'

He waited in the east wing. At first he couldn't pick her out. If she was there she was hidden by flocks of rowdy school children surging in from Golden Gate Park, their running shoes squeaking on the polished floors. When he noticed her she was breathless and a little dishevelled, her face pink and anxious. In the daytime she was as small as a child.

'Your cover is very good this morning,' he said.

'Shoosh.' She took his arm. 'Show me your work.'

And a month later he was not only out of New York, and over his lack of certainty, and ensconced in her apartment on California Street, but a bewilderingly fond step-father sitting cross-legged on the floor singing *I Have a Little Dreydle* and *Chanukiah Li Yeish* with Paul's third-grade class celebrating Chanukah.

The months passed happily with Linda on California Street. He worked all day in a sunny room on the roof with a view to Twin Peaks, the Fillmore and Japantown. In the afternoon tendrils of fog clung to the urban valleys. From his roof the tenements and terraces of the Western Addition were a Mediterranean vista of pastel pinks and greens. A sharp Australian sky stretched above the slivers of mist and, bisecting the distant streets, the Panhandle was as green as Africa. He could have been anywhere.

His income and travelling decreased (he travelled no further than Mendocino, San Diego and Los Angeles once or twice) but he was content having opted, finally, for art.

However, from that first morning at the exhibition—which had led to lunch, and a drink at the apartment while she collected Paul from Brandeis-Hillel school a block away, and to the first faint glimmering of an idea, an answer—his memory revived two impressions which became, after the terrible event, the clearest dream. And, he would believe later, a sort of augury in reverse.

The first impression was of the big elongated white marble statue of Saul, the first king of Israel. Saul is sitting back in his armchair in front of the museum's east wing. His mien is severe. Giggling, jostling schoolchildren prod his cold toes and scream. His feet. The feet are huge, well-shaped, precisely sculpted by (says a small plaque) William Wetmore Story (American, 1819–1895). The feet, in fact, dominate the sculpture, like the disproportionately large hands of Michelangelo's David. And the feet are deader than marble.

It's in front of Saul that they meet, that he finally notices her fair fringe and bright mouth on the same fringe and lip level as the boisterous children. Her face is rosy and intent. They link arms and move inside.

And abruptly the children break ranks and rush past them, and past an annoyed guard, into the African, Oceanic and American Native Art section where, dominating the end of the east wing, stands an Alaskan cedar-and-paint totem pole, the second image of his sharply revived memory.

The children have thrown off their teacher, their supervisors, the guard, and hurtle down the corridor—the squeaking of their sneakers turning the blood cold—towards the totem pole. They join it, press up against it, and it seems to absorb them into its savage layers: an eagle, a walrus, a lynx, a wolf, a grizzly bear holding a screaming human by the legs, all resting on a lurid foundation of some sort of sea monster.

The pole looms and grimaces, rocks at the children's prodding, and he pulls Linda urgently from its threat into the alcove which displays his quiet drawings.

# 11

When I stop the time at—or, rather, wind the clock back to—8 p.m. on 16 February, 1984, Linda Silver is thinking of nineteenth century Russian composers.

While it is 8 p.m. in Long Bay prison in Sydney, and Lawson/Levinson and I are drinking at the Sheraton Wentworth and waiting for the jury's verdict, it is, as I've mentioned, still 5 p.m. at Treasure Point.

Colonel Tripwire is, as earlier described, lying face down in the still-warm sand pretending to be the corpse of an Australian infantry private.

And Linda Silver, now Mrs Leon Lawson, is leaving her assistant Tracey to lock up the T-shirt shop and starting home to get ready for the open-air concert that night by the London Philharmonic Orchestra.

With Russian composers on her mind she wheels herself to her car, a Toyota specially fitted with a hand-controlled accelerator and brake, opens the driver's door and, with a practised buttock-hop, lunges from the chair and on to the driver's seat. Flicking a switch, she folds up the light-framed wheelchair and pulls it into the car after her. Despite her nimbleness this effort, in the present heat, makes her flushed and sticky. As she drives home she wonders suddenly, not for the first time, how she can possibly feel such a subtle sensation as the prickly dampness gathering between her legs.

How unfair that only the most unpleasant or painful sensations manage to defy the weighty numbness. Occasional menstrual cramps, for example (but, alas, no compensatory orgasms), ghostly arthritic foot pains, cystitis. Linda prays that the moist prickliness which she should not be able to feel is sweat or mucous or blood and not her bladder playing up again.

'Not my bladder playing up again' is not a phrase one normally hears from an interview subject, perhaps only from a disabled person with such a hard-learned detachment and frankness. But it was an indication to me a week later that her recall of her sensations that evening was complete. For some reason it was very important to me to get the full picture, to know exactly what was happening at Treasure Point at that time.

'It was an important evening for me and I didn't want my body to ruin it,' she recalled.

So, time is wound back. It is the evening of the London Philharmonic Orchestra's performance of an all-Russian program in a West Australian vineyard, and of her return to journalism. Having convinced the editor of its cultural and historic importance, she is to review the concert for the Treasure Point *Advocate*. Optimistically she sees it as a foot in the door or, in her case, a wheel in the door. It is—feet are inescapable here—a step forward. Linda is excited at the prospect of regaining something of her past entireness.

At home she washes, changes clothes and eats a quick snack while glancing through a book on composers and worrying vaguely about being a sham. (While a music lover, she is by no means an authority, she confessed to me, on Moussorgsky or Borodin. But she convinces herself she can wing it. Wasn't she the great improviser?)

Then, just before leaving for the concert, she prepares her body for any emergencies of incontinence.

And, as always, it is strange. The procedure makes her feel both a baby and a woman. As she is adjusting the pad between her legs she vividly remembers a similar action and its results, an off-stage excitement of a different sort, and one in which the subject of music again hung in the background.

This time the music was rock 'n roll and she was an English groupie, a band follower soon to be arrested for smuggling half a pound of 'pure' into America in her sanitary napkin and trying to sell it to a narc in a Long Island motel.

Here was the prime example of the honest con, of deceit in the cause of truth. Because she was unknown to criminals and police on the East Coast she had been hired by the Nassau County District Attorney to investigate charges of warder brutality and corruption at the Nassau County jail, one of several private investigators provided with criminal identities and imprisoned.

Wheeling herself out to her car on the hot and innocent side of the world she is suddenly quirkily nostalgic for her days of subterfuge. The heroin in the Kotex. The risk. The search. The physical abuse. This had been the role of her life.

Certainly her cover had had to be perfect. Her life depended on her secret. Neither the warders nor the prisoners could know she was a spy. While the narcotics detectives could brief her on the finer points of the heroin trade such as street prices and distribution techniques her problem was that she was obviously not an addict. Fellow prisoners might expect to see 'tracks' on a courier. But she'd reasoned that the prisoners would only be familiar with heroin dealing at the nickel-bag street level, not with the import trade, so she'd chosen the cover of an English groupie.

Her story, she remembers clearly, was that she'd dealt a little grass, some acid and so on, and had gotten involved with a bass guitarist who pushed heroin. Naturally an English rock musician would be searched by Customs, and even later, so she'd brought it in for him and been caught because she was out of her depth.

Out of her depth. The non-user caught with the stash. Being out of her depth had been consistent with her role at the beginning. Because she was pale and small and English and post-hippiesque in those days, at least in spirit, she'd drawn on her own personality of the sixties, the shy but radical English flower, and it had carried her through the four weeks in jail and the physical molestation and helped the Grand Jury indict twenty-four prison guards with corruption.

What she hadn't expected was that when she was released, her assignment successful, she'd be more out of her depth than her creation the groupie drug courier, disoriented, left almost as alienated by four weeks in jail as any long-term convict. And recognising the classic symptoms of prisoner neurosis hadn't helped her condition. Pointlessly angry at everyone she passed on the street, contemplating shoplifting at every counter, she'd drunk and smoked compulsively just to stop herself stealing lipsticks from Macy's and berating strangers.

It was after recovering from this restless state that she had, on returning to work in San Francisco, asked her agency for more defence investigation work and committed herself to prison reform and so set in train various expectations and events which led her to be here tonight.

# 12

In Sydney the lights in the metropolitan remand centre of Long Bay went out at 9.30. The prisoners, including those on remand and on trial, had been locked in their cells since 6.30.

In Sydney the jury was still out. Four blocks from the court Levinson (as I prefer to call him) and I ordered another bottle of wine with our dinner at the Sheraton Wentworth.

Outside Treasure Point (where it was still 6.30) a cloud of insect repellant hung over the stage which had been erected on the winery lawn for the performance of the London Philharmonic Orchestra. Crowds of casually dressed music lovers, many carrying coolers of domestic champagne, wine and beer, were arriving and settling themselves noisily on the gently sloping lawn which backed on to the acres of dusty earth and massed ranks of grape vines. Directly in front of the stage, in a reserved section fenced off and guarded by T-shirted ushers, flushed men and their wives, in evening dress, with gold badges signifying their status as special guests, were seating themselves.

Between these two groups, representing neither the Establishment nor the people, but the press, sat Linda in her wheelchair.

On the cover of her program she had already surreptitiously noted an argument between the musicians, which she'd overheard on the winery steps while waiting to be shown to her place, over performing in the heat.

She'd written: *Irate violinist (bald head shining with sweat): 'I'm not going on wearing tails! It must be a hundred bloody degrees out there!'* She'd then jotted down: *Murmurs of assent from strings.* And then: *Principal double bass: 'We must wear them. We must give the best show possible.'* Finally: *General mutters and moans.*

And now the members of the orchestra, tail-coated as always, were taking their places on the stage to great applause. Linda noted that the tuning-up was not easy. She jotted down: *Heat plays nasty tricks with strings.*

The day's shadows were lengthening as the conductor took the podium to cheers from the audience sprawled on the grass and to polite clapping from the reserved section. As he raised his baton and the concert began with Mikhail Ivanovich Glinka's fast-paced overture to *Russlan and Ludmilla,* Linda noted: *Strings surprisingly crisp and lively. Meticulous detail here.* And as the music pierced the thick evening air the sun went down, the temperature fell slightly, and in the eucalypts bordering the lawn the kookaburras and parrots, territorial and competitive, started their dusk chorus.

The concert had been timed to begin with the setting of the sun. Nature had been taken into account. Linda was charmed by the effortless harmony of events. The air was an envelope of warm hypnotic suggestions. As usual the mixture in this place was eccentric and seductive, amiable and strange. She closed her eyes and let the re-interpreted intentions of the romantic Tsarist, the risk-taking strings, the cackle of the kookaburras and the sweet poison of the insect repellant settle on her.

But even now discomfort nudged her. The pad tingled between her thighs. She squirmed in her chair. Sooner or later, just like any man, even Leon had asked, 'And so, what happened that time in jail?'

They had been together perhaps three months, living happily on California and Laguna. It was after supper, a cosy domestic scene. Paul was asleep. Leon was reading the *Examiner*. One of her cases was in the paper: Elmer Johnson was seeking a new murder trial. She'd been out at San Quentin interviewing him the week before, looking for the usual 'mitigating circumstances' for which Californian law made allowances. She'd told Elmer his timing was wrong. Wait another six months. She was in and out of jails all the time. San Quentin. Folsom. The City Jail.

'What do you mean, what happened?'

'The time you smuggled the heroin in the sanitary pad. On Long Island.'

'You mean physically?' I was body-searched of course, rather roughly, by a policewoman. She found the stuff. That was the whole idea, you realise.'

'No, I meant *inside* jail. When you were a prisoner. For four weeks.'

She wasn't taken with the look on his face that night. It was an unfamiliar look, a weary though self-protective look, as if he was already detaching himself from her answer. The *Examiner* rustled in his hands; he snapped it shut.

'I was seeking a particular kind of evidence.'

It was his quizzical look at this sentence that infuriated her, that made her exclaim, 'Yes, I was raped. The guards were corrupt. That's what we were out to prove and we did. And the bastards went to jail.'

They were both breathing heavily. He dropped the newspaper on the floor and held her by the shoulders.

She felt bitter all over again. 'It's all right,' she said. 'I was comforted later. By the women. *Convicts.*' He said absolutely nothing. His inability or refusal to respond hung in the air.

'Let me say something,' she went on. 'I've been raped and I've been mugged and rape's nothing.'

---

In her review Linda praised the millionaire winery owner for transporting the great British orchestra across the world to perform in a remote place in the open air before thousands.

She praised the musicians for participating in this novelty and performing under uncomfortable and unusual conditions. (She cited the example of the cellist who had insisted on carrying his instrument all the way to his seat on the stage in its heavy case: 'Do you know how old my cello is?' the cellist said. 'Two hundred and ninety-one years. It's worth $65,000. I must look after it.')

She mentioned the 'surprisingly lively and crisp' string playing in Glinka's *Russlan and Ludmilla*, its 'meticulous detail.' She said that Moussorgsky's *Night on the Bare Mountain* had afforded opportunities for 'colourful tonal combinations' from the wind section and she approved of the 'appealingly distant' flute solo in the work's final stages.

The conductor, she noted, had given the musicians much freedom within a 'flexible yet disciplined framework' in Tchaikovsky's *Fifth Symphony* in E minor. And 'rhythmic urgency' had been rightly the keynote in Borodin's *Polovtsian Dances*.

Then she gently pointed out the shortcomings of the performance.

# 13

After Linda had been pistol-whipped in 1978 while serving divorce papers in the Pink Palace, a housing project in the Fillmore district, an interviewer for *New West* magazine asked whether the tension of personal danger, the Smith and Wesson on the bedside table, ever got her down.

She answered that of course she was now more cautious than she used to be. 'I used to think God was on my side and that I was somehow magically protected.'

The 1978 article had two photographs of her. (Her fringe covered the remaining bruising.) There was one taken of her target shooting, with the caption: 'It's really quiet and Zen-like on the pistol range. It's as gruelling as a ballet workout.' She looked sleek and determined, holding her gun in that double-handed steadying grip favored by television cops. In the second picture she smiled warmly in front of the mantel in her Columbus Avenue office. On the mantel—a nice shamus touch—was a *Maltese Falcon* statuette.

In the photographs she didn't look like someone worried by danger. Nor did she sound worried, despite the recent mugging. She sounded philosophical. 'I could have drowned in the rage I felt,' she admitted, 'but I *was* in the wrong part of town, alone, white, after dark. And divorce makes people go crazy.' However, she assured the interviewer, she wasn't so much of a masochist that she'd ever go back there.

I read the *New West* article in her scrapbook at a wrought-iron patio table at Treasure Point in late February 1984. She'd insisted there be no more publicity, no more stories, nothing on the record, no names, no addresses. But she brought out her press cuttings at Levinson's suggestion and rather proudly pointed out the interview, which began:

> Of course she is a crack shot. In the best traditions of hard-boiled detective fiction, Linda Silver's life is one of personal danger, existential loneliness and daily subterfuge.

We sat in their verandah's shade overlooking the Indian Ocean. Low glassy waves swelled around the point. Heat glanced off surfaces and a watery mirage hung over the glaring rim of the sand dunes. Linda's quotations leapt out of the press clippings at me.

'It's more *pure* work than most people do,' one quotation enthused. 'It's intellectually fascinating and enormously liberating to do something that scares you and have it come out all right.'

Another quotation likened a good investigation to a well-turned piece of furniture. 'Everything fits together beautifully,' she said. 'Facts and procedures flow into logical conclusions.'

Moreover, she said that in her work she always looked for an answer that cut through the chaos to utter simplicity. 'I call it the *elegant solution*.'

I looked at her over the patio table, across a terra cotta saucer of tiny cactuses and other dun-colored succulents. An awning rattled in the wind. In the garden hot air whipped each blade in the dry lawn towards the sea. I indicated the article. 'The *elegant solution,* I like that.

She fidgeted in her wheelchair. 'Hmm'. She seemed slightly embarrassed. Her pale legs, straight and smooth as pencils, slanted on to their little foot-rest. 'Funny thing, logic,' she said.

# 14

In one type of puzzle based on the continuous line
your pencil joins the dots one to two to three and so
on and perhaps discovers a giraffe. In another, the pencil
has to negotiate a maze of traps and blind alleys before
it reaches home.

A child's puzzle hint: if you don't want to go over
the edges, if your aim is a free-flowing and continuous
line, it's easier to travel through the maze in the opposite
direction. Begin at *Home* and work your way back to
*Start.*

The Castles' party by the Swan River at which Spargo
and Levinson were the celebrity guests was the *Start* of
this story. And Treasure Point is the end. Treasure Point
is *Home.* But everything really began at *Home* when
Spargo discovered the *Fortuyn.*

After 16 February, 1984 it was imperative to me to
follow the trail, all the trails, back from Treasure Point.

I already had Levinson's version of the reason for the
flight from California. After midnight on the night the
jury was out he'd finally revealed why they were lying
low in the town created by Spargo's discovery.

And Linda? On their verandah at Treasure Point she
eventually gave me her version. I don't put the reason

down to my persuasive reporting technique so much as to the fact that her new reviewing job had somehow broken the ice. She, like me, was working her way back from *Home*. I think she also still hankered after the *elegant solution*.

So I learned this from both of them.

The voice on the inter-com downstairs had said two words, 'Linda? Franco.' Franco was a colleague at her agency. She said, 'OK,' and pressed the button that unlocked the door from the street into the lobby.

It was still early, almost 8.30. They were finishing their coffee and watching a talk show. The guest was a famous feminist author. It was a flirtatious interview; the host and guest wrinkled their eyes at each other and innuendo flew about the studio. The elevator stopped at their floor as expected, the door opened and then clashed shut.

'Look at her fiddling with her skirt, doing all that business with her knees,' said Linda. She was laughing as she walked down the hall to answer the apartment door to Franco. The buzzer was calm, not insistent at all, and it surprised Levinson to hear the indignant note in her voice when she opened the door to her colleague.

The talk show host was farewelling the feminist author while giving the impression that off-camera it wouldn't be goodbye at all but supper at Elaine's, when a male voice shouted, 'Sign it!' and a gun went off and somewhere Paul screamed.

In a long corridor of time the gun kept going off while Linda screamed and Paul screamed and the hysterical male voice was yelling at an eerie pitch. During these endless seconds Levinson rose from the settee and kicked over his coffee and the TV host riposted to the feminist's final wisecrack, and by the time he was on his feet and remembering the Smith and Wesson in the bedroom, the man was between him and the bedroom anyway. But Levinson kept running heedlessly into the moonlit hall as the man ran out of bullets—having emptied his pistol into Linda's body—and stepped over her and burst out the door.

The man had a thick beard and a woollen cap on his head. The black man with the gun. Black like Franco, but not Franco. The elevator door clashed and closed, the mechanism made its familiar hum as the elevator went down—he could hear it through the open door—and behind the horror, back in the living room, the TV host was still signing off as if nothing had happened.

Linda was seeping patches of blood through her sweater. The patches grew quickly and in the moment he was on the phone they joined together and spread over the whole sweater and down over her jeans.

She was crying and clutching her stomach. Paul was standing in his bedroom doorway, white and rigid. 'I love you both,' she cried. It was like being in a film, or a dream, being conscious of reaction to action. Levinson acted and saw himself acting.

'I'm dying,' she cried in his arms. 'It hurts. *I didn't do it.*'

The ambulance arrived faster than its siren. The ambulance was outside and the paramedics were thumping up the stairs like an army before he heard the siren.

'Outa the way, fella,' they said. The medics were as big as the policemen, young footballer types with similar authoritative belts jangling with keys and tools. They strapped Linda, bleeding Linda, strangely conscious, on to the stretcher and connected her to tubes and bottles and bore her away. One of them holding high a bottle of fluid ran alongside as they carried her vertically down the stairs. The top of her pale ruffled head was the last portion of her to disappear.

218

*I didn't do it.* What was that?

The sirens were still blaring, even building in crescendo, as he and Paul were led downstrairs and swept up in the noise and spinning lights and carried away.

# 15

As we know, Linda didn't die hearing sirens. She remained alive during the dash to hospital and through the tranfusions and emergency surgery.

She survived a total of five bullets: one in her spinal cord and large intestine and bladder, another in her chest, two more in her upper right arm and one other which grazed her right temple. The sixth missed her entirely.

She thought it was anger that had kept her alive, frustration at being wrongly maligned. She believed her body was protesting at being forced to die misunderstood.

'I didn't do it!'

Didn't do what?

Her attacker had ordered her to sign a sheet of paper, a declaration which said, 'I betrayed Elmer Johnson and the entire prison reform movement when they needed me most. May I rot in hell as a sell-out capitalist opportunist.'

'Sign it!' he'd shouted, this 'Franco', pointing the .38.

'But it's not true!' She couldn't sign it, anyway, without something to lean on. Leaning on the hall cabinet, the gun waving and shaking only four or five feet from her, she had scrawled her name. Then he shot her, again and again (One bullet was embedded in the telephone directory.) She thought she heard the snap of the bullet through her spine. ('It sounded just like clicking your fingers,' she recalled.) Then, imagining she would surely die, he ran out the door.

'I didn't do it. Betray them.' These were her first words to Levinson a week later. She was gaunt and whiter than the sheets. Tears ran down her cheeks.

'Don't worry about that.' She was alive. What did her 'confession' matter? It was signed under duress. A jailbird's fantasy. What moron would think it had any legal or moral standing anyway? Just a piece of paper, a signature, childish propaganda, simple emotional symbolism. How could anyone take it seriously?

'Don't worry about it.' But people were worried. Linda was placed under twenty-four hour guard at the hospital. The Department of Corrections had heard whispers that her attacker was a member of a 'revolutionary' prisoners' group which used paroled prisoners to carry out reprisals for political slights, real or imagined, against those inside. 'The Black Guerilla Family.' A police guard was also placed on Levinson and Paul for two days. Then they were advised to move out of the apartment.

'Hide out for a while,' the police said. 'Lie low, just like in the books. We haven't got a handle on these guys yet. They probably want to kill you.'

They moved to North Beach first. For both their sakes he rejected the idea they were hiding, telling Paul they were moving to be closer to the hospital. They moved into, and under, the home of some friends, Dan and Beth Hogarth. The Hogarths had the small middle apartment in an old three-story building on Mason Street between Columbus Avenue and Fisherman's Wharf. Beneath the bottom apartment, below street level, was a storeroom which Dan, a documentary film editor, used as a cutting-room and office.

'Truly, you couldn't get anything more private or cosy,' Dan said. The room had a divan and a camp stretcher, seagrass matting on the floor, and on the walls were posters and souvenirs of the Hogarths' travels.

After dinner upstairs, Levinson and Paul headed, exhausted, to bed, down the back wooden staircase to the storeroom. The neon sign above the Doggy Diner on Columbus threw bright light on the back porch as they said goodnight, but as they went downstairs the yard got gradually darker.

Levinson felt his way along the black corridor beside the building, holding Paul's hand and drawing him after him. The little boy was too tired to whimper. There was a strong smell of dog urine and he wished he could see where they were treading. Above them in the light loomed the scaffold of the staircase. He realised they were whispering but couldn't bring himself to speak aloud. At the end of the corridor, beyond the doorway to the street, there was a muffled noise of traffic, the scrape of passing feet, a snatch of conversation. He fumbled the key into the lock and opened the door into a cavern of even deeper darkness.

'Not in there!.I don't want to go in there,' Paul cried.

He hushed him and found the light switch. At once the storeroom looked welcoming enough, though smaller than by day. He put Paul to bed on the divan and lay beside him. The boy soon fell asleep, literally fell, dropping from plateau to plateau in a series of twitches and shudders. His lips murmured, his eyelids flickered and even when he was fast asleep his eyes eerily remained slightly open, as if watchful.

When Levinson turned off the light the room was thick with darkness. He lay back on the divan. There were no windows; he had noticed a small ventilator opening into the black corridor and through it wafted the faint odour of dog piss. He had difficulty breathing. He lay on his back with the boy's hair touching his cheek and tried to sleep.

A curse woke him. A black man's oaths. Was it a dream? Footsteps boomed in his ears and a thin light fell on his face. His chest felt caved in with terror. Then he woke fully to fractious laughter, more restless footsteps above him, and the sound of TV commercials, sentences of old movie dialogue, the belligerent switching of channels.

'White trash,' a man's voice growled.

A TV voice was repeating an item from last evening's news: of anti-nuclear demonstrators marching on the White House. He recalled the images: banners, beards, babies. Toothy effigies of Jimmy Carter. He looked at his watch—2.30 a.m. The tenants of the ground-level apartment had returned home. Their floor had no carpets and the light shone through the cracks between their floorboards into the storeroom.

The blacks roamed directly above, shouted at each other, scuffled, poured drinks. He heard every restless sound. The weary aggression seeped down into their hiding place. And punctuating the testy hubbub was a strange tapping noise and an intermittent frenzied scratching, relentless and continual, tapping and scratching.

If he could hear them so clearly surely they could also hear him and Paul. He willed the boy not to wake, not to murmur in his fitful sleep. He was unwilling himself to breathe in case they picked up his wheezes. And now his bladder ached. Overhead the feet stamped; the men cursed; further away the television blared a string of late night commercials for discount carpets, furniture, kitchen settings; the dog—it had to be a dog—tapped across the bare boards on its nails, stopped and scratched itself frantically, then resumed its weary pacing.

This was the oldest of nightmares dredged from race memory and brought up to date. Americanised. Lying in their dungeon, trapped and passive, Levinson wept quietly for Linda and them all.

But the body has a way of intruding, of forcing its demands over all others. Gradually the insistence of his bladder overcame his fears of discovery, overtook even his more fanciful flights of terror. He eased himself off the divan, alert to every creak of its springs, and crept to the door. If Paul woke, missed him and cried out, they were lost. Outside, he crept along the corridor and, in the yard already reeking of dog, urinated for what seemed like hours.

Back in the storeroom, easier in body if not in spirit, he collapsed on the divan. The people above were quieter now and he eventually fell asleep.

# 16

They lay low in North Beach for three days. Each night Levinson's nightmares were disturbed by the homecoming and fractious roaming of his neighbours and their itchy dog. He woke with a start to curses in his ear, scratching, the bellowing of TV spruikers. Each night he hardly dared breathe.

By day Paul and he ventured outside only to the playground in Washington Square, to the tourist-crowded anonymity of Fisherman's Wharf, to the Safeway on Chestnut and Columbus. By day the Goodyear blimp watched over them. At night the Doggy Diner sign lit their unwilling steps downstrairs.

Every day they inspected files of photographs and video lineups of suspects. No face jumped out at them. Their man was black, bearded, stocky, wearing a woollen cap. So were half of these people.

Then the police were tipped off that the doctor who had prevented Linda from dying was going to be killed. Levinson was shocked at this mad logic.

'Out of town's got be safer for you two,' the police told him.

The doctor walked out of the operating theatre, closed down his practice and went to Europe. Linda's guard was increased. Levinson and Paul moved out to a rented house in Marin County below Mt. Tamalpais and hid in the woods with the Smith and Wesson.

George Silver was there, hungover, on special leave from Harvard, to share the news three weeks later that the police had arrested someone for Linda's attempted murder. The police had asked Linda and Levinson if they could identify one Edgar Franklin, 29, in a video lineup. Linda said she thought that of the seven men in the lineup he 'looked most like' her attacker. Levinson identified him positively.

'That's Linda!' George said. 'There's such a thing as being *too* fair. He had the bloody gun after all.'

Buckeye branches scraped on the roof. Wind hissed down the chimney. George, Paul and Levinson ate take-away tacos; the men drank Napa Valley red wine; Linda Silver's males all together in the rustling woods, hiding, consoling each other and willing her recovery.

George said, 'What benefit of the doubt did those crazies give her? Those dumb terrorists? No thought, no intellectual analysis. OK, granted they've got an axe to grind, the blacks've had a bad deal, old story, prison's no picnic, I take the point.' His indignant English accent carried through the bare, echoing house. 'What I'd like to know is by what perverted twist of logic do they decide to kill a sympathiser! A bloody friend!' He took a draught of wine and it caught in his throat. 'She was always too good for this country,' he gasped.

At the preliminary hearing of charges against Franklin, Sergeant Gregory Acronico testified that the (clean-shaven) ex-convict had been arrested near the intersection of Hayes and Steiner streets after he and two other under-cover narcotics agents had observed him and another man smoking a marijuana cigarette.

When the officers had identified themselves, Franklin

had jumped into the street, pulled out a handgun and screamed, 'You're not taking me to jail!' After a violent scuffle he had been arrested. The .38 pistol was found to be the gun used to shoot Linda Silver five times at close range.

According to Sergeant Acronico, Franklin's briefcase contained a list of names, home addresses and home telephone numbers for foreign diplomats, as well as an underground bomb-making manual, two pistols, a stop-watch, surgical gloves, two thousand dollars traced to a Bank of America holdup and photographs of the power plant at Folsom prison.

'It is our belief,' the sergeant testified, 'that the next stage of their plan was to kidnap foreign diplomats to force the release of certain inmates at Folsom.'

In quiet Marin there was no fractious pacing and cursing above his head to wake Levinson at night, but in Marin, even after the arrest, he could still hear rustling in the bushes. Things still coughed in the woods.

At Franklin's trial the defence attorney emphasised the point that Linda's initial identification of her attacker had not been positive. A dermatologist testified for the defence that Franklin was unable to grow a thick beard like the one Levinson had described. An astronomer declared that there had been no moon—hence no moon-light could have clarified the gunman's features for Lev-ison's benefit—on the night of the shooting.

In obvious pain, Linda appeared in her wheelchair to give evidence. The defence attorney did his best to recover from this blow by alleging that it was precisely because of her terrible injuries that the witnesses felt bound to lay the blame on Franklin.

The jury deliberated for ten hours and found him guilty.

At that second, and ever after, Levinson was sure they were wrong.

It was over, but he found his nights changed forever. For Levinson thereafter, every night in America, at Treasure Point (even, I suspect, on the night in the Sheraton Wentworth in downtown Sydney on 16 February, 1984), there was rustling in the bushes and something coughing—or perhaps it was a muffled oath, a snatch of fractious laughter—in the woods.

# PART THREE
## Discovery

# 1

When the police car reached the station on the night of Spargo's and Caroline Castle's abortive rendezvous at Shark Bay Spargo was taken immediately to a cell without being charged.

As he walked inside someone struck him again on the head from behind. He faced them, ready to fight, but they all stood back. As he turned again one of the constables threw a shovel of sand over him.

At 9.30 next morning, without food or drink, he was brought directly from the cell into the neighboring court room to appear before the local justice of the peace. The J.P. was a grey-haired woman with a kindly face; he recognised her as the matron of the district hospital. Her desk was flanked by three policemen; another two blocked the exits. The prosecutor was a sergeant whose voice and manner he remembered from the fight at the hotel.

The J.P. looked up from her desk. 'Yes, sergeant.'

'Your Honour, the prisoner stand accused of resisting arrest.'

'How do you plead?' asked the J.P.

'Not guilty.'

The sergeant confidently outlined his case. The accused had been arrested on the authority of a bench warrant issued a year ago. Bail had been estreated when the accused fled the state. Now he had returned by boat in company with others with some nefarious plot in mind. When apprehended at the hotel he had resisted with violence and it had been necessary to use fifteen men to restrain him.

(He made no mention of the ballast-brick charge which had caused the affair.)

'That's not true. The facts are . . .' Spargo began.

'Keep quiet!' ordered the sergeant. One of the policemen placed his hand on Spargo's shoulder.

The sergeant leaned over the J.P.'s desk and, whispering, prodded at a page in a book he pushed in front of her. 'No, not that one, this one,' he muttered. She frowned, then nodded and looked up at Spargo with a relieved expression.

'I find you guilty as charged and sentence you to six weeks,' she declared.

Considering that this jail sentence was the point when Spargo was confirmed as a criminal, first by the police, then by the press and the social network—and lost his last vestige of popular support—the reaction of the law was double-edged. At the enforcement end, the police would hound him even more; at the theory end, the High Court, after pondering his application for several years, would eventually see his side.

As Rosanna reminded me in late February 1984, a summary of official charges against him would have to include Detective-Sergeant Russell Sikes's charging him with the ballast brick offence the moment he was released from Fremantle jail.

The charge was thrown out of court.

Sikes then charged him with unlawfully using explosives on the *Fortuyn* wreck. (Case dismissed.) Sikes charged him next with unlawfully selling coins from the *Fortuyn*. (He was convicted and fined.) Sikes charged him with blowing up the pirate statue at Treasure Point. (Acquitted.) Details of his numerous prosecutions for traffic offences are too trivial to mention.

The next official charge was conspiracy-to-murder. The unofficial charges against Spargo, far more actionable in some eyes, can be summarised in the name Caroline Castle.

# 2

Journalism imposes its own forms of order on the world's, the nation's, the town's events. It imposes its forms of order on both the facts in a story and on the arrangement of stories itself. Its aim of course is to draw the reader's attention to what in the day's or week's happenings the editors deem most important.

Naturally this violates the larger truth of a chaotic universe. But, as it happens, readers also make their own editorial judgements, their own hierarchical arrangements. They may easily ignore the editors' prescription by dwelling on, say, the story of the rapist on page thirteen instead of the company takeover on page one.

They are casting a vote for the larger truth of a chaotic universe.

What is interesting is that every now and then the editors are likely to join the ranks of the readers. For a schizophrenic moment they can be imposing their forms of order on the world's events and simultaneously throwing them out the window.

Take the story of the rapist on page thirteen. A judge has just awarded a convicted rapist a large sum of money after deciding that a road accident has limited his ability to enjoy sex.

The accident victim had a twenty-year history of attacks on women. He was injured by a car while jogging (he liked to keep in shape); the driver was culpable. The judge mentions that injuries to the man's arms meant that he could no longer support his weight during intercourse. He could no longer assume the dominant sexual position.

Awarding him compensation, the judge says that the injuries had severely affected the man's enjoyment and way of life.

Around their desks on the 'quality' broadsheets, the editors and sub-editors discuss the story, laugh and snort cynically. The story amuses them, annoys them, supports their personal view of the legal system, of life, whatever. The story engages that part of them that is the general public. For a moment they become honorary readers, participants in the chaotic universe. And then it's back to work; they become serious professionals again; they reimpose their order on events and relegate the compensated rapist to page thirteen.

On the day the story of the compensated rapist languished on page thirteen (or fifteen or eleven) across the country, the Castle Corporation's takeover of National Transport Industries was featured uniformly on page one. The takeover was described as 'shrewd and skilful', approving adjectives usually applied by the finance writers to the business manoeuvrings of Peter Castle.

(The finance writers also had the habit of referring to each new takeover as 'the latest Castle coup', conjuring up visions of a medieaval seizure of power. They did not, however, customarily question whether 'the latest Castle coup', depending as it did on borrowings of millions of dollars from overseas banks, had added one cent to the nation's wealth, was in any way advantageous to the community or had, in fact, added to the foreign debt.)

On 13 September, 1979, three days after the story on 'the latest Castle coup', there was a four paragraph item under a one-word heading on page seventeen of *The West Australian* which, despite its brevity and placement, went further than most people could remember towards revealing the larger truth of a chaotic universe.

While indirectly connected to 'the latest Castle coup' it definitely collided head-on with journalism's forms of order. Moreover, it managed to engage the interest of the general reader to an extent perhaps only possible in such an isolated and self-contained city.

It is appropriate to quote it here:

### OBITUARY

Mrs Caroline Jane Castle, wife of the Castle Corporation chairman, Mr Peter Castle, was found dead yesterday in their home in Jutland Parade, Dalkeith.

Mrs Castle, the mother of a son and daughter, had been in ill health for some time. Previously she had served on the committees of numerous charity organisations.

Mrs Castle was the daughter of Mrs Margery Frame, O.B.E., of Peppermint Grove, and the late Mr Ernest Frame.

Police said there were no suspicious circumstances. Funeral arrangements will be private.

———

Such stories break all the usual rules. They are newspaper nightmares everywhere. However, a new set of emergency rules are quickly handed down. Pressure bears down from above. The industry that depends on regular crisis for its existence is suddenly vulnerable in the face of a small domestic tragedy.

Pressure is applied on two fronts. First, the actual words are subjected to concerted attack. Every word of the awesome item is minutely examined and re-examined as if such wishful scrutiny could literally wipe the page clean, expunge the event. The reporter's original story, the actual sheet of paper, travels all around the newspaper building, back and forth from the messy newsroom to the mahogany executive suites. At every stopping place it gains little scribbled marks—nervous deletions and brave, agonised additions and then nervous deletions once more—from ballpoints and pencils and managerial fountain pens.

Then the people are put, or put themselves, under similar pressure and scrutiny. The reporter may even be regarded suspiciously for supplying this troublesome news. An atmosphere of 'shoot the messenger' may prevail. The chairman is telephoned at the club. The managing director leaves his dinner party. The board members telephone and are telephoned. The editor has more contact with management in one evening than in a whole year of elections, wars, cyclones, assassinations and economic recessions.

And at the coal-face, the exposed seam, the reporter waits for them all to exhaust themselves, trying not to feel guilty for having ruined their evening or, worse, for having created this monstrous event in the first place. And when time, the deadline, finally brings the panic to an end, he or she is left with only a *Who?* and a vague *Where?* and *When?*

The *Why?* and *How?* have disappeared.

———

In that gem of brevity, the story of 13 September, 1979 headed OBITUARY, even the clues, the code, the journalistic euphemisms, were decidedly oblique. For example, 'found dead' generally translates as sudden death (probably violent), but 'had been in ill health for some time' usually means cancer. On the other hand, 'police said there were no suspicious circumstances' means suicide.

The social network's bush telegraph, at least for the first twenty-four hours, was only guessing. In any case it didn't know the newspaper code. But it did have that extra knowledge which enabled it to read between the lines. It made its own connections.

And it certainly knew its own cultural habits. It noted with surprise the presence of police. It focused on the 'funeral arrangements will be private.' It pronounced suicide. An untidy suicide.

---

Of course there was a more precise *Where?* and *When?* The *Where?* was on the bed in the guest bedroom, on top of the covers, in—there was reasonable certainty on the part of the policewoman present—a burgundy silk camisole (clinically, even brutally, chosen), while Benny Goodman and the Boston Symphony playing Mozart's Concerto for Clarinet and Orchestra in A Major smothered the *pock* of tennis balls and the imperious instructions of the tennis coach correcting Jon Castle's backhand on the court below.

The coach's time was valuable, he told the police (and would later tell the closed inquest); young Jon's tennis lessons began at four and they had just started. Notwithstanding Benny Goodman and the Boston Symphony Orchestra, the coach confidently estimated the *When?* at 4.07 p.m.

And the *Why?* Do suicide notes ever satisfactorily

explain the *Why?* Does it help to read that the writer couldn't 'go on any longer', that her 'faith in the human race' had been 'shattered,' that every time she heard a 727 fly overhead it was carrying nuclear warheads? That she couldn't shop in town any longer because the traffic noise on Stirling Highway sounded like invading tanks?

The *Why?* in this case needed no note, though the note Caroline Castle had positioned safely on the dressing table (gracious in its failure to name any of those faithless humans) did thoughtfully serve to establish the 'no suspicious circumstances' required by the police.

The *Why?* in the case of Caroline Castle was perfectly answered not only by her chosen method, its symbolism and the self-perception inherent in that choice, but by the firmness of purpose necessary to bring it off.

Only by assuming the foetal position could she insert the barrel of the shotgun up between her thighs and manage to reach the trigger.

The *How?*

# 3

One of the facts which the news item headed OBITUARY omitted to publish was the surprising discovery of a three-hundred-year-old Spanish coin embedded in the shattered plaster of the wall above the guest-room bed.

Owing to the secret nature of the subsequent inquest, this fact still didn't see print even though the coroner's attention was directed to it.

The finding of an eight-*real* piece minted at Seville in 1685 amongst the lead shot in the wall at a suburban death scene in 1979 had aroused official curiosity to the extent that numismatists, quickly summoned, had within an hour sourced it to the *Fortuyn* and consequently to Spargo.

Another court case. But who would have imagined the pain of this one? The disapproving voice of authority.

"Have you seen this before?"

He tried not to look as it was placed in his unwilling palm. Once more it fell and rested on his damp skin. A shallow U of metal, bent and shiny in its wounds. It balanced in his hand.

"Would you closely examine the coin and tell the court how it came to be in Mrs Castle's possession?"

This pocked and eroded piece of Peruvian silver which

had lain at the bottom of the sea for hundreds of years and between her breasts for sixteen. In its time twice part of the earth's structure. Both ore and coral reef. Concreted and swept by the sea. Caressed by her salt, too.

His impulse was to squeeze the bent coin, cup it in his palms. But never to look at it. And in the cold court, in the presence of her implacable husband and family, his eyes focused and blurred first on its specks of plaster dust, his mind brimming with fatal trajectories, grisly lines of flight, and the deafening explosion of possibilities.

Then, of course, the rusty particles he'd been dreading, the minutely clotted lettering around the edges, filled the shambles of his imagination.

I imagine.

He'd had to leave forever this time. The old Thirsty Point, the city, the two-and-a-half million square kilometres of the state were too constricted for him. He took up with Rosanna—quiet, young and anonymous—who had no past and was the centre of no rumors. Maybe she'd worked in an office; no-one enquired. He left with her for the east. They drove across the Nullarbor Plain, preceded and followed by his reputation for trouble.

However, there was, she believed, literally, a silver lining.

'He carried a swag of pieces of eight with him. He also had some old Phoenician coins, ancient Chinese money, bits of gold and so on.'

He also had the favorable High Court decision, which meant that he must be compensated for finding the *Fortuyn* and having it taken from him; four million dollars had been mentioned.

She recalled them being followed by a police car in Adelaide. They were stopped by police as they came into

Melbourne. The sergeant who searched their car in Melbourne said something about stolen gelignite.

*The six-stick man.*

When he found nothing he inspected their driving licences, took down details and allowed them to drive on.

---

The headaches on the Hume Highway.
You ok?
He shook his head slowly.
Pull over. I'll drive
Must be the headlights.
I'll drive. You sleep.
Walking around the car, weak-legged, feet slipping on the gravel shoulder. A dog barked miles off. Dust and rubbery fumes over the highway. His brain pushed down on his eyes. She moved behind the wheel. As she drove off he had one hand to his eyes, the other to the side of her freckled face, against her young kind ear.

You sleep.

---

The headache continued down Parramatta Road into Sydney past the motels and used car yards and fast food stands. In town she headed directly for St. Vincent's in Darlinghurst. She had a sister who was a nursing nun.

'Not a word,' she said. 'I know where to take you.'

She parked on a taxi rank, took him in, booked herself into the Koala Motel. A week of tests: a C.A.T. scan, electroencephalogram, angiogram, explosions in the head. A week of valium sedation. In three days he felt fine, ate all his fruit and bonbons, beat her easily at Scrabble.

'Nothing physical that we can detect.'

He had friends in Sydney, and knockabout acquaintances. The Marriotts put them up when he came out of hospital. But it was the knockabout acquaintances whose company he sought in the Leichhardt and Five Dock pubs every evening, adventurous men who undertook challenging tasks for money.

He began behaving recklessly in drink. He sold his *Fortuyn* coins in hotel bars: twenty, ten, five bucks each, as if they'd fallen off the back of a truck. Argumentative, he was easily slighted and quickly maudlin. When he got into fights he hit hard and early and left before the police came.

At least one of his knockabout cronies was actually performing challenging tasks for the police, but he discovered this only later.

He shouted:

I'm the famous fucking skindiver. I'm the famous explorer. I've stood underwater shovelling bullion into bags till the sweat ran through my wetsuit. I'm the famous six-stick man from W.A. I am *all right* now. They can't do any more to me.

He yelled in bars that he'd changed laws and redirected history. He was brighter than they knew, he shouted. *Qui cherche trouve.* And he fucking had. He was as dogged as buggery.

No one here (he would challenge), no one in this hole of a pub is aware of Victor Hugo's novel *Les Misérables*. Well, you dumb bastards, I'm Jean fucking Valjean.

Three nights in a row he started fights, won them and was put into cabs weeping, taken home by patient Marriott to the pregnant Rosanna.

Nervous exhaustion.

# 4

Does it matter whether you believe in an editor's view of events or in the larger truth of a chaotic universe?

Does it matter which line you follow? Or that the line might stop abruptly and for no known reason?

Levinson made one remark while we waited in the Sheraton Wentworth for the jury's decision that I remembered even during the dramatic events of the next twenty-four hours.

He said he regarded Spargo with both gratitude and anger. He was grateful to him for having introduced him to Thirsty Point back in 1962 when he found the *Fortuyn*. He was quite content, he said, to live the rest of his life there screen-printing crayfish on to T-shirts. He thought of his father, his vests and socks, the same business.

'At least it keeps the parentheses open,' he said.

Faced by my incomprehension he mentioned a conversation with Spargo back then, while they camped on the beach under the trailing edge of the sudden cyclone.

'We were drinking rum one night to ward off the gale, or I wouldn't have been so patronising. At least that's how he took it. I told him that fame, even my little slice of it, had taken a toll. I described the feeling I'd

have whenever a book of my work was published, whenever I saw my drawings in an exhibition or my name
in a catalogue.'

I imagined Spargo, chuffed and ruddy with his success,
squatting with his cup of rum in the lee of the bottle
heap, hearing of the drawbacks of borderline celebrity.

'I said I felt I was becoming an abstract biography.
My life was neatly enclosed by parentheses. It was terrifying the way my existence was beginning to appear
in print, like a waiting gravestone.'

He'd complained that his birthdate was always followed by a hyphen: *Leon Levinson* (1920—      ). His
death day was left open. The dash hinted at the end
so eagerly awaited by all the art historians and librarians,
all those cold vultures—*Not long now, folks.*

'They couldn't wait to fill in the gap. The essential
thing to these people was that I be placed between parentheses. I couldn't be let free.'

Levinson looked at me over his drink. Then he suddenly spluttered into laughter. 'Do you know what
Spargo said? "Fuck your hyphen, Leon. I'm unstoppable."'

I saw the picture very clearly. I remembered walking
with Spargo from the Supreme Court to the Palace Hotel
when he'd said, 'Who do they think they're dealing with?'

But at the same time I remembered my surprise when
he brought up Caroline Castle's name in the front bar,
his fingers nervously shredding a drink coaster. 'She
always has tears in her eyes.'

A conflicting element in these recollected remarks
would cloud the particular version of the night's events
that I would prefer to believe next morning.

Journalism followed the official line. The newspaper
version kept to the facts. The jury had still been out.
The jury was still considering whether Spargo and
Rosanna had conspired to kill Natalie. Spargo had been

alone in his cell since lockup at 6.30 p.m. The lights in the metropolitan remand centre had gone off at 9.30.

At 5.30 next morning he was found by the warder who brought his breakfast. He was hanging by his sheet from the bars of the cell window. The sheet was blue, jail-issue, twisted into a three-foot rope. He was wearing only a singlet and underpants. His chair was lying on its side under his body. On his head was a bump where it had apparently struck the window ledge. He had died at approximately 8 p.m. There was no note in his type-writer, or anywhere. No one had heard anything.

It wasn't stated until the inquest made it official, but the implication in the heading *Explorer Found Hanged in Cell* was clearly suicide.

# 5

Levinson and I knew nothing of his death when we attended court, nursing our hangovers, next morning. All day the jury remained out. After deliberating for thirty-two hours the jury finally filed back into the court room at 7 p.m.

Rosanna entered the court then, assisted by Butterworth, her lawyer. A policewoman held the baby. Rosanna's face was puffy. She looked overcome by the strain of waiting for the verdict. Even Butterworth was pale and distracted. We were surprised at Spargo's absence.

The judge asked for the verdict on Rosanna Marie McMahon first. The jury foreman rose and pronounced her not guilty. She showed no relief, surprisingly, at the news.

Then the judge called to the witness box an official from the Corrective Services Department. The official gave evidence that he had delivered a note to the judge that morning informing him of the death in prison of Donald Patrick Spargo. The members of the jury sat stunned. Two women burst into tears.

The judge apologised to the jury for keeping the news of the death from them, but said it would have been impossible for them to continue their deliberations had they known.

'You are discharged from returning a verdict on Mr. Spargo,' he instructed them.

Rosanna had been told, of course, early in the morning, and directed to keep up a pretence for the good and proper working of the jury system.

The law allowed itself an exquisite irony here, one not lost on Rosanna, on the sorrowful Butterworth, on us, or on the row of detectives, barely able to contain their satisfaction, in the public gallery. The jury had actually delivered a sort of phantom verdict on Spargo. Without the jury revealing their intended decision, without their saying a word, the court knew that they would have acquitted Spargo. How? Because the charge was conspiracy. The judge had reminded the jury that it took two people (at least) to conspire. Both defendants, or neither, had to be convicted. And Rosanna had been found not guilty.

Had he lived, Spargo would have been set free.

Unfortunately, legal principles didn't allow for that to be made official. The jury's verdict could not be announced, nor his name cleared.

As we left the court and I hurried back to the office with this news event I remembered asking Levinson the night before, 'What did he do that made you angry?'

'He took me for $10,000,' he said. 'A loan, he said, to pay his legal expenses for one of his other trials. You know, the statue bombing. Ha!'

'He wasn't himself after the Caroline Castle inquest,' I suggested.

'That's why he bombed the stupid pirate,' Levinson said.

# 6

Whether correct or not, the version of Spargo's death which I believe is his version.

It's his version whether it's the true version of what happened (as I further believe) or just what he wanted everyone to suspect had happened (even if it hadn't). Either way, it's the version he had been consciously and unconsciously creating since 1962; no, earlier—since the week after Easter Sunday 1957 when he'd found the *Fortuyn* and then lost it.

Not surprisingly it bears a slight resemblance to the nightmares he described to Rosanna, to the re-creation of a dream.

The cell reminds him of a diving bell. It's the last night. They can't really leave it any longer without taking the gamble that he'd be freed. He would be most surprised if they didn't act tonight.

He is alone, of course, and in his underwear for bed. The night is humid but not hot, not scorching like his hometown. The Perth newspapers, with their full coverage of the heatwave and meagre coverage of their trial, he stacks on the floor 'out of the way,' he thinks.

The cell doors are locked at 6.30. The lights are still

on. There is no more need to work on his case. For a moment he thinks of the next day's possibilities and his pulse throbs in anticipation of the verdict.

Sitting on his bunk he feels only metal and stone around him. Time passes but he doesn't read or rest or even lie down. There is still an opaque milky light outside his window, the distant city.

Perhaps an hour later there are firm, quiet footsteps at his door. It opens and three men come in. He doesn't get up. These are the men who control his life line, the unnamed, faceless people who operate the winch, the air supply. Who periodically dictate events. He held off fifteen men once, tonight he stays sitting on his bunk until he is really definite (though he's sure he does know) what they want.

'We've got something for you to sign,' one says pleasantly. 'For court tomorrow.'

'You'll probably get off too, you lucky bastard,' another says.

He looks. It's a blank sheet of paper. He shakes his head. They don't bother to argue. One of the men steps up and hits him on the head with a truncheon. When he falls forward off the bunk they take the sheet from it and twist it into a rope, make a big, looping noose at one end and tie the other to the window bars. Breathing heavily, they lift him up on the chair, two men passing him up to the third, who stands on the chair and places the noose around his neck before stepping down.

The laugh is they think he's out to it when they're setting him up there on the chair with the sheet around his neck holding him upright. He isn't. The light is bright. The cell is a diving bell. The laugh is the four million dollars of High Court settlement willed to his baby, his daughter of the trial, of all trials. The laugh is they've bungled it: the bump on the head, the lack of a note—and he'd never sign off in his singlet and underpants. Who'd believe it of him?

He's not out to it. Not when they kick the chair away and all his body moves to his throat. *Roar!* Oh, Caroline, the wild sparks! The brilliant teeming plankton in the air! My heart is red at my throat. My brain, my black breath is yours.

# 7

She saw the colors and light and unusual lines.

The pink sky beaming in the west. The limestone headland in position in the east. Tomorrow's optimism gathering in the red sun.

While there was just enough blue in the sky I rolled over the side of the boat, he told her.

He described how the ocean was calm and clear to the bottom. He dived down to the reef without a thought, his body repeating its familiar motions. She saw his fins waving against the current, the slanting silver line of his air bubbles. The air in his mouth, her mouth, tasted of rubber. The sea was surprisingly shallow.

Perhaps it was the particular light, the accidental precision of his alignments, the currents, or all these things, but peering through his misted mask he saw instantly in front of him the tubular coral outcrops poking from swollen humps on the reef. When he scraped at one with his knife it flowered with rust, bulbous blossoms under the coral and anemones, and from inside its barrel a tiny agitated rockfish shot out.

He could have shouted and sung underwater to find one cannon. But there was another, also with its angry little resident, and, further along, an anchor. Suddenly

Nature was full of straight lines and perfect circles and the unnatural brassy flash of verdigris. And at the edge of the shelving reef, on a ledge piebald with the presence of metals, he found what looked like hundreds of small scattered bricks.

He was rising excitedly to the surface, his mask half knocked from his face and filling with water, when he saw another protrusion curving out of the reef, and he pulled at it, snapped it off and carried it up with him.

All the way to the top, he told her, I couldn't stop laughing at the idea of finding an elephant's tusk here at the bottom of the sea.

Robert Drewe
**The Bodysurfers**

'His short stories are front-page featurettes transformed by poetic vision.' TIME

'His characters repeatedly hurl themselves at life and lovers. There is something very powerful and poignant in these stories.' NEWSWEEK

'A remarkably seductive and exuberant collection which manages, in its portrayal of human relationships, to be both mordant in tone and playful in manner.' THE TIMES LITERARY SUPPLEMENT

'These stories breathe. Taut yet teeming with life, seductive yet stylistically chaste, they are shot through with gritty phrases that catch at one's throat.' SYDNEY MORNING HERALD

'*The Bodysurfers* is a brilliant book. It is clever, touching and at times desperately funny.' CANBERRA TIMES

Robert Drewe
**The Bay of Contented Men**

'Robert Drewe is masterly...one of Australia's most original writers, exploring contemporary culture and identity in ways which keep exposing new angles of our uneasy repose.'
HELEN DANIEL, SYDNEY MORNING HERALD

'This is writing at the highest level of narrative achievement, a book which deserves international acclaim and respect.'
JIM CRACE

'Crystalline, taut and accessible... While Drewe's stories are beautifully lucid and direct, they are crafted with a highly sophisticated narrative technique.'
ROD MORAN, THE WEST AUSTRALIAN

'Comic in a deeper sense than that realised in the jokes and flashes of wit. Content, hope, or at least a dignified refusal to despair, is wrung out of this grim world – and that's a triumph of the human spirit.'
TIM KELLY, THE AUSTRALIAN

'It would be a mistake to presume to understand Robert Drewe too quickly...There is a sense in which he is writing in the Country of Last Things, waiting for the End...'
DON ANDERSON, THE AGE

# Robert Drewe
## Our Sunshine

*Our Sunshine* is the tale of a man whose story outgrew his life.

Robert Drewe, whose fiction is acclaimed for holding a mirror to contemporary suburban Australia, has now taken the country's greatest mythological character and created his own imaginary life for him. He presents an unsentimental, compassionate and sensual portrait of the boy and killer who became both the National Hero and the Devil Incarnate of the Antipodes.

Succeeding in turning myth to funny, savage, commonplace and back again, Drewe portrays Ned Kelly and his adolescent gang both as young Horsemen of the Apocalypse – riding through Fire and Flood, Sex and Death – and as the psychologically displaced victims of the casually brutal human wilderness.

Drewe not only gets inside the boy and man who thereafter embodied Australians' best and worst perceptions of themselves, but shows the crazy instability of the early days which created the Australian legend.

The stunning clarity of his prose carries us into a dreamworld of astonishing and violent revelation, an entrancing and frightening landscape of murder, prejudice, sexuality, persecution, robbery, vanity, religion, greed, politics and corruption...a world which we must finally recognise as our own.